THE KNIGHT BEFORE CHAOS

ENIGMA SERIES VI

TIERNEY JAMES

Books by Tierney James

Enigma Series
- An Unlikely Hero
- Winds of Deception
- Rooftop Angels
- Kifaru
- Black Mamba

Stand Alone Novels
- Turnback Creek
- The Rescued Heart
- Dance of the Devil's Trill

Wind Dancer Series
- Dark Side of Morning

Education
- African Safari

Education for Marketing
- How to Market a Book Someone Besides Your Mother will Read

Children's Books
- There's a Superhero in the Library
- Zombie Meatloaf
- Mission K9 Rescue

PRESS

Owasso, OK

ISBN-13 978-1-965460-20-7 (Paperback)
ISBN – 13 978-1-965460-21-4 (eBook)
:

DEDICATION

To my little kiddos who generate joyous
chaos at Christmas and throughout the year. You
are my heart.

ACKNOWLEDGMENTS

Now is the time I get to brag on all those people who keep me on track and encourage me along the way. Without you I may have given up a long time ago while trying this writing life. You make me better every day. Thank you for believing in me and loving my work.

Paperback Press – Without your guidance and ability to move mountains, I probably would still be on the first book. Your words, "Don't stress this. I got it," is music to my ears during the roughest times.

Wizards of Publishing – Thank you for always seeing the good in my words and finding value in what I do. Your guidance to being a better writer is done with skill, kindness and humor.

Lipstick & Danger Street Team – All the work you do for each of my books, still amazes me. Time after time you give me advice, get the word out about my books, appearances and so much more. You are so important to what I do. Thanks for never giving up on me.

Family – My family means to the world to me. I'm so blessed God has put each and every one of them in my life. Some of the antics you see happening in my stories, actually is a version of the real thing. Things are never boring in my life.

CHAPTER ONE

The car skidded on the slick road, causing the three passengers to squeal with childish delight. Captain Chase Hunter did not share in the jovial mood, since he'd been assigned this particular mission of retrieve and rescue for his agent Tessa Scott.

"Awesome," Sean Patrick, the oldest child, cheered before landing a fist against Chase's arm. "Where'd you learn to drive like a badass? My mom teach you?"

Chase could feel his brow pinch in irritation at the suggestion the boy's mom could teach him anything. Well, maybe how to handle three rambunctious kids would have been a good idea. Talk about being at the wrong place at the wrong time.

The snow had started a few hours earlier, flurries at first, and now he could only use the low beams on his car to see the road clearly. He didn't want to be responsible for kids, especially these kids. He'd rather walk on burning coals with the Taliban in hot pursuit than do this job. Now he could hardly see the road and second-guessed whether or not he'd secured the two in the back in their car seats he'd removed from his agent's SUV. Sean Patrick was buckled in next to him, but he kept pulling the belt forward to loosen it.

He could imagine slamming into an out-of-control truck after slip-sliding on the freshly fallen snow. The next image was the kids lying facedown in the snow with blood pooling under their heads. Tessa would never forgive him. No. She would kill him if anything happened to her angelic monsters. Even now, he could almost hear the wheels of mischief turning in their underdeveloped brains. Had he ever been in this kind of danger?

"Can we play Christmas music, Chasey?" Heather, the youngest, chirped from the back seat. Before he could answer, she burst into a chorus of "Jingle Bell Rock." With a glance in the rearview mirror, he could see her moving back and forth in her car seat, the flaps on her unicorn hat flopping with each new verse. Her sweet voice softened him enough to smile.

"Don't call me Chasey," he demanded.

Sean Patrick turned to smirk at his little sister. "Yeah, Heather. Call him Badass."

"I'm tellin' Mom you said ass," Daniel, the middle child declared. Chase adjusted the mirror to see him cross his arms on his chest and raise his nose in the air. "Dr. Hunter is more appropriate."

Sean Patrick mocked him by repeating his words in a baby tone.

"Enough, boys. Call me Chase."

"The church is up ahead—Chase." He pointed to the right.

He pulled into the back row where all the other cars had shied away. Even after removing the key, Chase sat for a few seconds and surveyed the surroundings. Spending the last few years in Afghanistan had instilled a heightened sense of awareness of his surroundings. First, he took note of the roof of the church then the cars already parked. When Sean Patrick clicked out of his seat belt, he threw his arm out to hold the young boy in place.

"What?" Sean Patrick lowered his head to mimic the way Chase watched the falling snow. "We're goin' to be late," he informed Chase as the others escaped their restraints.

Chase nodded, opened the door, and quickly moved to the passenger door to assist Heather. The snow had accumulated to at least six inches, and the boys decided a snowball fight was in order. He reached in and lifted the little girl in his arms, but before he could set her feet down, she circled his neck with her arms. Her little face came so close, he couldn't help but see the resemblance to her mother. The dimples appeared when she smiled and patted his cheek.

"Will you carry me, Chasey? I don't want to get my boots wet."

"Spoken like a real diva." Chase chuckled as he locked the car door. "Boys," he scolded when Daniel hit him in the back of the head with a snowball. When the wetness fell into his collar, he pivoted and leveled a warning glare at the boy.

"Oops. Sorry, Dr. Hunter. I meant to hit Heather."

He wanted to be irritated, but Heather cleared away the snow with her little gloved hand. Like her mother, she had him wrapped around her finger.

Sean Patrick darted through the parking lot, periodically kicking up snow and tumbling into the snow, accidently on purpose, Chase guessed. To try and halt the activity would only encourage a lie or more rambunctious behavior. It hadn't taken him long to evaluate the oldest of Tessa's kids. This one had mischievous written all over him. He also barked orders to his siblings. The kid might be practicing for an officer position in the Army.

By the time they reached the front door of the church, both boys were splattered with snow. They walked in, stomped their boots on the rug, and peeked into the sanctuary where an organist played "Joy to the World." He kneeled down to help Heather out of her parka and removed her hat, revealing a lot of smashed strawberry-blonde curls, another likeness to her mother. The temptation to push her hair behind her ears became too great for the soldier as he toyed with one of her curls.

"You look pretty tonight, Heather." Chase stood, and the little girl slipped her hand into his.

"I don't want to go in there." She looked up at him with pleading eyes, round and afraid.

"Why not? Your mom said you're supposed to sing a song for the play. She'll be so proud of you. Your grandparents are coming all the way from Tennessee to hear you."

"I'm not very good." Her bottom lip stuck out.

"You sang all the way here. You were amazing."

"Katie Shoemaker says my voice sounds like a rooster crowing."

A tall girl about Sean Patrick's age moved to the front of the sanctuary. She smirked at Heather then put her hands under her armpits as she let out a loud crowing sound. Heather came to a screeching halt and leaned into Chase.

"Shut up, Katie Shoe Leather," Sean Patrick yelled. He pushed his nose up to resemble a pig's and snorted his way to the front of the church, twisting and turning like a farm animal. Daniel laughed so hard the choir director turned to see about the commotion. The kids already on the stage laughed, too.

Chase's opinion of Sean Patrick went up considerably.

"Don't listen to that brat, Heather. She's jealous of your beauty and talent." He patted her head then stroked her cheek. "She's a bully," he whispered. "Stand up to her."

"I'm scared," she mumbled, continuing to stare up at him.

Some of the parents were engrossed in visiting instead of watching their kids get into place for practice. He chewed the inside of his jaw and continued to scope out the sanctuary for problems.

"Boys, come here," he called to her brothers. They hurried up and hugged their little sister. "Take your sister to her place. I'll sit here until practice starts. I'll move to the back in a few minutes. Good job taking up for her, Sean. Proud of you." The boy puffed out his chest a bit.

Sean Patrick took his sister's hand. "Come on, Tooki." He smiled at her as Daniel took her other hand.

"I'll sit by you and help if you forget your lines." Daniel shoved his glasses up on his nose.

"Thanks, boys." Chase scooted into a pew. "I can't wait to hear your song, Heather."

She looked over her shoulder and offered a sad but angelic smile.

He gave her a thumbs-up. "Show no fear."

The mean girl ran up to a beefy young boy in his early teens and whispered in his ear while pointing at Sean Patrick.

"This can't be good," Chase mumbled.

The two boys found Heather's place, but the choir director refused to let Daniel sit with his sister. They both offered some words of encouragement before moving to their seats.

When Daniel started to sit down, the beefy teen jerked the seat back, and Daniel landed on the floor. When Sean Patrick's face turned to a mask of anger, he jammed a fist into the attacker's shoulder. Laughter broke out among the other children.

Before Chase could scramble out of the pew, both boys were

rolling on the floor, their grunts accompanied by yells of stop by the choir director who took a spill trying to separate them, and other children laughing and urging them on. All the while, the redheaded girl sat with her arms crossed on her chest and an evil smile stretching across her freckled face.

By the time Chase jerked the director up by his collar, the older boy had gotten the upper hand on Sean Patrick. He easily separated the boys and held each at arm's length. Sean Patrick struggled to get free and land another blow, but the pastor showed up, clapping his hands for order.

"What is going on?" he demanded.

"This guy thinks it's funny to jerk a chair out from a younger, smaller kid." Chase released him so fast, the boy staggered back into the pastor.

"Sean Patrick is kind of a bully these days." The pastor looked down his nose. "Since his mother isn't around as much, the Scott children are a bit of a handful."

Chase glanced out at a few of the mothers who appeared to be all ears then back at the pastor. He stuck out his hand. "I'm Chase Hunter, a friend of Mrs. Scott. She asked me to bring them to practice. She is stuck at the airport."

"I need to speak to Sean Patrick about his behavior for a few minutes." The pastor pointed to the music director. "Go ahead and get started."

Sean Patrick stared down at the floor and sighed, probably used to getting called on the carpet.

Chase nodded. "Well I'll go along to make sure I can inform his mother of the conversation." The pastor hesitated, and his eyes rounded a little too much for Chase's liking. He slipped a hand on Sean's shoulder and squeezed. "We're buddies, aren't we, Sean Patrick?" The boy looked up at him in surprise but quickly nodded. "I would be remiss if I didn't come along."

"Have it your way. Come on."

"Aren't you going to take the other kid?" Chase glanced over at the bigger boy and noticed a smirky grin.

"My son and I will talk about the incident later."

"He's your son?" Chase laughed, drawing a frown from the pastor. "Figures. The preacher's kids are always the worst ones in the church."

"Excuse me?" the preacher huffed.

Chase laughed again and patted Sean's shoulder. "No offense. I'm the son of missionaries and a holy terror." His laughter stopped, and he arched his eyebrow. "Guess I still am. Or so I'm told."

The introduction to the music cantata began as the pastor motioned for his son to follow after all then led them into a room off the sanctuary. A crash sounded at the far end as the pastor flipped on the lights. An elderly man with a bloody head fell to the floor as two others froze like deer in the headlights. Scattered coins and greenbacks left no doubt as to what had taken place.

Although one man wore a ripped jean jacket, Chase quickly spotted tattoos on his neck and a knife in his hand. The taller one hunched and reached into his tattered coat pocket.

They stumbled back when Chase rushed them. He landed an uppercut to the knife guy's throat, dropping him to the floor as he elbowed the other's nose, grabbed his free hand, and twisted it so he dropped to his knees. Chase quickly relieved him of a pistol before pounding him to the floor and placing his boot on his neck.

"Well, you guys are going straight to Hell. Robbing a church at Christmas? What were you thinking?" The knife guy tried to get up but got a swift kick to the gut. "Get me the extension cord over there, Pastor. Will you call 911?" In seconds, the two Christmas burglars were hogtied.

He focused on the injured man as Sean Patrick ran to his side and kneeled by him. "This is Mr. Cooke. He's my Boy Scout leader." Sean Patrick's voice quivered as he spoke. "Is he going to be okay?"

The sound of distant sirens mixed with concerned voices from the sanctuary. Several mothers entered to check things out only to gasp and hurry back to make sure the children remained calm. Police soon arrived, along with paramedics. Chase had already evaluated the injured man and tried to reassure him he would be fine. The paramedics confirmed the good news before the police pulled Chase aside. Two other officers took the would-be burglars out the back door to keep from scaring the children in the choir. He tried to keep an ear tilted toward the boys while the pastor talked to the police.

"That guy is awesome. Where did he learn to do all the kung fu stuff?" The preacher's kid now engaged Sean Patrick with the appearance they were old buddies. "Who is he?"

Sean shrugged nonchalantly before speaking. "He's my personal trainer. Teaching me how to fight without fighting. You know. All the ninja training you see on Assassin's Creed. I think he invented it."

"No kidding!" The teen stared at Chase in awe.

He asked the police officer to wait a second then moved toward the boys with a deliberate narrowed stare at Sean Patrick. "You boys okay?"

"Yes, sir!" the teen blubbered. "You getting those guys was about the coolest thing I've ever seen. You got those guys good."

Chase shifted his attention to Sean Patrick who watched the police before he turned a challenging gaze toward him. The kid reminded him of himself at about the same age, openly defiant, and unafraid of the consequences. "Sean Patrick?"

"I'm good. Nice moves there, Mr. Badass."

Chase narrowed his eyes to slits. "Watch your mouth."

Sean Patrick grinned as he saluted him. "Yes, sir. I was tellin' Luther you been teaching me some of those moves." His voice slowed as if he might be trying to send a message.

Chase lowered his head and eyed Luther. The kid wasn't much different than a green recruit shifting with unease at the scrutiny. He nodded then offered a fist that Sean immediately bumped with his own. "Yeah. He shows a lot of potential."

The teen eyed the younger boy with a new appreciation. "Sorry about being mean to Daniel earlier and fighting with Sean Patrick. My sister is such a tattletale. Dad says I should take up for her."

"Tell her to stop making fun of Heather." Patrick rolled his shoulders and straightened. Chase wasn't sure if he should laugh or give him an atta boy.

The teen seemed to take offense at the demand. But, to the bully's credit, he stole a look at Chase, who decided to arch an eyebrow and cross his arms across his chest.

"Sure, Sean." He stuck out his upturned palm. "No hard feelings."

Sean slapped it but remained stoic. "No hard feelings."

The choir director stuck his head in the door and motioned for Chase.

"What's the problem?" Had Sean Patrick committed an infraction toward another person?

"It's Heather. She refuses to sing her song unless you and Sean are there to listen. I even let Daniel sit by her, but she's having none of it."

"Okay. Be right there."

Chase eased into the front pew as Sean Patrick took his place on stage. He smiled at Heather and Daniel like a conquering hero, adding a pat on the head to each of them.

The organist played the intro bars, and the director cued Heather when to begin. She waved to Chase, walked up to the microphone that had been lowered for her, and sang "Silent Night" in a sweet little voice. Something inside him lurched, and he touched the spot over his heart. It usually ached when her mother walked into a room. He pictured Tessa when she was a little girl. Why did he feel so powerless around these two females?

One minute he was staring a hole in a burglar and thinking about doing an adjustment in his ability to walk upright, and the next he couldn't stop smiling at a little curly headed girl with the voice of an angel. He suddenly realized the existence of a God. Being with these children might be a test of endurance and patience, but maybe in a small way he could redeem himself for all the suffering he'd handed out over the years.

When she finished, Chase stood and applauded and cheered. Apparently, the timing in showing admiration needed some work because the music stopped and everyone looked his way. A few of the kids snickered, the director appeared confused, and the organist rolled her eyes. But Heather bowed and curtsied princess style before she stepped cautiously off the stage. She ran to him with outstretched arms. He scooped her up to receive a grateful hug.

"Awesome!" he praised. "You'd better go finish your practice." When he set her down, she kissed his cheek, and scampered back to her place. "Dear God in Heaven. Help me through this night," he mumbled.

CHAPTER TWO

Chase pulled into the driveway and stopped the car before letting out a sigh. He rubbed his face. The sound of seat belts clicking and excited conversation about the choir misadventures forced him to admit it wasn't so bad being the hero to a bunch of little kids and a holier-than-thou minister. It remained difficult to keep from turning into a marshmallow with Heather tugging on his hand as they walked up the front porch steps.

Their mother, Tessa, had hired someone to install the Christmas lights and greenery around the Victorian country-style home. Even the yard glowed with white lights, giving it an almost Hallmark vibe with red bows attached to swags of greenery on the porch railing. He spotted a sled and faux gifts on each side of the red front door. He wondered about the time and effort it took to make the holiday magical. Clearly, Tessa wanted everything to resemble a magazine cover.

The magical feel evaporated once he opened the front door. A stiff breeze smacked them in the face from an open window he spotted in the dining room. Snow dusted the hardwood floors and the trestle table laden with open boxes of Christmas décor. A few boxes lay sideways, and several Santas with broken arms and an occasional busted head lay scattered across the floor.

The Scott children froze at seeing the mess that continued

throughout the cozy living room. A bare tree reached to the ten-foot ceiling and showed signs of leaning a little too far to the right. A number of clear ornament tubs remained stacked in front of the sofa with cushions and pillows in disarray.

"I smell something burning," Daniel declared as smoke alarms pierced the air. He stepped forward, only to be pulled back by Chase. He should have brought his weapon but had decided watching three little kids would not require extreme intervention. Another miscalculation on his part.

"Stay here." Chase moved toward the kitchen, but the children grabbed onto his coat hem and followed. He glared down at them in hopes of putting them in their place, but they continued to stare straight ahead without picking up on his warning.

"I'm scared," Heather whispered then decided to circle his leg with her arms. Peeling her hands free only forced them up to his coat pocket where she latched on like a hungry piranha.

He instinctively laid his gloved hand on top of her head and stroked her silky hair as he walked into the kitchen. The microwave crackled with sparks, and a pungent odor filled the air. Chase quickly cleared the time left then grabbed the fire extinguisher he demanded Tessa keep under the sink after a mishap once before when she nearly burned the kitchen down. With the flames gone, he opened several windows only to notice the back door ajar.

"Mom is going to have a cow." Heather put her hands on her hips.

"Not too bad." Chase examined the door and wondered about fingerprints but decided there were probably many grimy little traces of the kids. To go through it wouldn't be worth the effort. "We'll have this cleaned up in no time. Looks like our visitor stuck a piece of aluminum foil in there to slow us down."

"So, he was here when we came into the house?" Sean Patrick asked, his eyes wide with shock. "Wow. This is turning out to be an exciting evening."

At the stomping of feet running across the upstairs floor, the children jumped toward Chase. He patted their heads then headed for the steps, telling them, "You kids hide in the pantry and don't come out until I tell you." They stared at him with wide eyes. "The pantry has a lock on the inside at the top. Sean, I think you can reach it. Don't come out until I tell you. Scoot."

The boy grabbed his siblings and rushed them toward the pantry as instructed. Chase waited to hear the click before slipping upstairs with the Walter P90 pistol Tessa hid on top of the china cabinet in the dining room. Not even her husband knew she owned one. After some unsavory threats toward her and his Enigma team, he'd taken it upon himself to help her choose the right weapon for self-defense and to show her how to use it. She'd been a quick study and felt confident in her ability to protect herself and her family. Of course, this one was unloaded, with no ammo to be found.

Another cold breeze tunneled down the hall from the master bedroom. The door moved back and forth on its own. Someone grunted as he plowed into the room with his weapon drawn. A dark figure flung itself out the window then slipped on the snow-covered roof and propelled off onto the ground below. A loud thud and groan followed. With caution now in the wind, Chase secured the weapon in the inside pocket of his jacket then followed. He sat down to glide along the same route as the uninvited guest without doing himself any harm.

A fleeting memory of when he'd escaped out Tessa's bedroom window during one of her training sessions surfaced. She'd passed with flying colors, no thanks to the surprise arrival of her husband, Robert. Chase found himself having to make a quick getaway, leaving his new agent to clean up the mess and create a perfect lie to cover their tracks. The man remained clueless as to what his wife really did for a living. Now he felt himself airborne once more and landed in a cushion of snow on top of the intruder.

He bounded up and jerked the man to his feet with a powerful grip. Giving him a shake, he committed the man's face to memory before doing a quick frisk. When he squirmed and swung his fist at his captor, Chase landed a blow to his chin, sending him flying back on his butt.

Something moved to his left, and he managed to dodge the full impact of a large branch, but it caught him on the shoulder. Staggering back, he snagged his foot in a string of loose Christmas lights that had fallen with the first burglar when he tumbled off the roof. The new attacker yelled at his partner to get up as he reared back to strike Chase.

Chase rolled away and sprang up when the heavier man's club shattered against the ground. He watched the man turn and run toward the neighbor's yard and found it amusing when both men attempted to jump over the fence and tumbled into an undignified pile. The prospect of an easy capture, especially since he carried a gun, quickly evaporated when a tree branch laden with wet snow dropped on top of his head. This gave the two a few extra seconds to disappear into the night.

Taking a deep breath, he shook the snow off like a wet dog then moved to the back door only to find it locked. So much for due diligence earlier. He'd secured the dining room window and the front door, and the kids were locked in the pantry. When he stuck his hand inside his coat pocket, he remembered he'd handed his phone to Daniel when he extinguished the microwave fire.

"This keeps getting better and better," he growled and dared eye the lattice on the outside wall near the master bedroom window. If he gauged everything right, he could climb up then ease onto the roof. At least the upstairs window remained open. He scrambled up the lattice until his foot smashed through a weak section, sending him down several feet before catching himself. On his second try, he inspected each rung until he reached the roof and easily slipped onto the surface.

"Whatcha doin', Chasey?" came the sweet singsong voice of Heather from the ground below.

"You know being up there is dangerous, right?" chimed in the sarcastic tone of Sean Patrick.

"I'm telling Mom you didn't set a good example for us," Daniel threatened. When Chase stood up to order them back indoors, his feet slipped out from under him, and he barreled toward the front edge of the roof.

To the accompaniment of gasps and a girly scream, Chase managed to catch hold of the gutter with one hand, leaving him dangling like a lopsided Christmas ornament. Then the gutter gave way, and he fell to the ground. The children quickly ran and kneeled beside him.

"Are you okay?" Sean Patrick helped him sit up.

"Why were you on the roof? I thought you went to see what was upstairs." Daniel along with his brother offered a hand to assist him to his feet.

A groan escaped from deep inside his chest, although he had no broken bones.

"Why are you outside?" he growled. "I thought I told you to stay in the pantry until I came for you. What if there was trouble?"

Sean smirked. "The way I see it, you were in trouble and needed us."

"I see you're snarky like your mom." Chase pointed toward the door. "Move."

"Was there someone upstairs?" Heather grabbed his sore hand and shivered.

"Probably a scouting party for Santa." He smiled down at her, and she clapped her hands and twirled. The boys opened their mouths to contradict his announcement until he leveled one of his death stares in their direction. "Those pesky elves. What'ya going to do, huh?"

Sean Patrick squinted and twisted his mouth into a snarl. "What about the mess down here?"

Busted. "That was a burglar."

Heather covered her mouth with both her gloved hands, and her eyes grew wide with fear.

"But he's gone now," he reassured her, squatting and helping her out of her hat and coat. "I'm here now, and I'll protect you. Okay?"

She nodded then circled his neck with a tight hug. "Okay." He tried to stand up, but she pulled him back down and gave him another kiss on the cheek. "I really like you."

He laughed and managed to pull free. "I kind of like you, too." With a slight pivot, he looked behind him. "Where's your brothers?" Before she could answer, he ran into the foyer and cocked his ear in hopes of locating trouble. "Boys?" he called, a little more irritable and louder than he intended.

They popped up from behind the sofa, somersaulted over the back, bounced on the cushions, and crashed onto the floor, laughing with abandonment. Had he ever felt the same kind of happiness as a kid?

Most of his childhood was spent in a dirty Chinese village with his missionary parents or with his ambassador grandfather in some hellhole in the Middle East or on an Indian reservation with his maternal grandfather. Many times, he was left on his own with only his little sister as a playmate or in the company of strangers who tried to entertain him for the duration of his visit. Then he'd be sent back to China to his parents who were doctors.

Once the giggling stopped, they leaned back against the sofa and pointed over their shoulders to the back of the couch. "There's a problem," Sean Patrick announced.

"No kidding." Chase surveyed the room and wondered how he would manage to do all the things he'd promised Tessa he'd do before she arrived with her parents. "That Christmas tree is pathetic. First, we're going to have to shore up the base. From the looks of all those tubs, there are more ornaments than room on the tree."

Daniel pushed his glasses up on his nose. "Mom is going to freak when she finds out all the presents she hid behind the sofa are gone."

"Guess that new security system didn't work." Heather walked in with her hands on her hips then shook her curly head. "Sure hope Santa comes through." She sniffed as her lip jutted out.

"No. No. Don't cry, Heather." Chase held his hands out, hoping it would stop the tears. "I'll fix this. I promise." But she opened her mouth and let out a wail he suspected would wake the dead.

CHAPTER THREE

Tessa sucked in her breath before easing down into a plastic chair. She switched the phone to her other ear as people rushed around her at the Reno-Tahoe International Airport. Christmas decorations sparkled everywhere, but a wave of panic washed over her while listening to Captain Chase Hunter inform her of the burglary.

"The police just left. The kids are fine. Heather had a bit of a meltdown when she thought there would be no presents."

"I don't understand. I checked out the security company." Tessa palmed her forehead in frustration.

"Police are looking into it. Had another complaint earlier in the evening. Then there was the problem at the church." She could imagine him gritting his teeth when things spun out of his control.

"Have the kids given you any trouble?" She wondered about the pause at the other end of the phone.

"Truthfully, running from the Taliban is a lot less complicated. The kids outmaneuver me at every turn."

She couldn't help but release a soft laugh. "You aren't doing it right. Let them know you're the boss and in charge."

"Heather is the worst," he moaned.

Tessa felt amused. "Aw. I'm so proud of her." Another moan. "Chase, you are being too nice, and Heather is worming her way into your heart and psyche."

"No kidding," he quipped. "Reminds me of you." His voice took on a growling tone.

"She manipulates her father and brothers like a magician. Don't let her get away with not helping out. And by no means let her snowball you."

"When will you be back?" he sighed.

"Yeah. About that…"

~ ~ ~ ~

Chase rubbed his face with both hands as he mulled over Tessa's words. "I won't be back until tomorrow."

"What?" he demanded. "You can't do this to me, Tessa."

Her parents' plane had been delayed in Denver, and they wouldn't arrive for another hour. The highway over the mountains had closed because of dangerous weather conditions. Robert, Tessa's husband, would be stuck in Chicago until tomorrow afternoon and hoped to be home by dinner.

"I'm so sorry, Chase. I promise I'll make it up to you. Really."

Chase considered her promise but knew they were not on the same wavelength when it came to redeeming anything he had in mind. "I'm going to hold you to that." Her soft laughter only made him long to see her smile. "Gotta go. One of your neighbors is headed onto the porch. Kind of a looker." His constant hope was something would eventually make Tessa jealous enough to end things with Robert.

"Probably Bridgette from two doors down. Might be right up your alley: divorced and horny."

"Call me later, Tess."

"Hello?" came a voice laced with a French accent. "Everything okay? Tessa?"

The front door slowly opened, and a lovely lady wearing a faux leopard jacket and hat, black leather boots, and leggings entered the foyer.

"Hello. You must be Bridgette." He extended his hand and noticed her delicate touch lingered a little longer than necessary.

"Yes. And you are?"

The kids came thundering into the foyer and slid to a halt next to Chase. Heather seemed to mark her territory by taking Chase's hand in hers then leaned into his side.

"He's Chase Hunter, our new babysitter," Daniel announced with a laugh. "So far, he isn't doing well."

"Yeah. The cops are on a first-name basis with him now." Sean smirked and elbowed his brother who laughed even harder.

Bridgette shifted her eyes from the children to Chase and slowly raised her eyebrows. "Really?"

He remembered Tessa's warnings and spoke firmly. "You boys get in there and clean up the mess you made." This time it wasn't a request but an order. He forced a stern tone that could command troops, not a bunch of snotty-nosed kids. "Now," he snapped angrily. The boys straightened for an instant then hightailed it into the living room.

Bridgette smiled. "Well, I must say, you can certainly take charge of rowdy boys." She glanced down at Heather. "Shouldn't you help your brothers?"

"Nope." She smiled, looking up at him with worship. "Chasey and I stick together."

He couldn't believe how much the little stinker imitated her mother when she got snarky. A ridiculous laugh spilled from his mouth before he turned his attention to the neighbor. "She's my helper and protector, I'm afraid."

"A big strong man like yourself doesn't look as if he needs any protection," she cooed, adding a wink.

Before he could respond, Heather pulled Chase down to whisper very loudly into his ear. "Mom says Bridgette is a cougar. I better stay with you to make sure she doesn't bite."

Embarrassment crept up his neck in waves of heat. A lame excuse for amusement escaped his lips when he stole a glance at an irritated Bridgette. "Kids." He managed to give her one of his killer smiles to soften her glare at the child. "Besides, the cougar happens to be my favorite animal."

"Well, mine, too," she said shifting her weight to one hip. "If you're sure everything is all right, I'll go home and light a fire." She winked again. "If you know what I mean."

Before he could offer some encouragement, Heather piped in, "Of course, he knows what you mean. We have a fireplace, too. See?" She pointed to the one in the living room that the boys had flipped on then she went to the door and opened it wider. "Thanks for stopping by. Mommy will be here soon. Chasey will take good care of us until she comes home. You don't have to worry."

If ever there was a human who resembled a ravenous bird of prey about to snatch up its dinner, it was Bridgette when she narrowed her eyes and glared down her delicate nose. Chase managed to step forward and pull Heather behind him. "Thanks, Bridgette. We had a break-in, and the police were here to take our report. Be sure you turn your security system on. Wouldn't want anything to happen to you," he suggested in a deep voice.

She stepped onto the porch and turned back. "Well, some things just happen, you know."

Chase wanted to respond, but Heather slammed the door before he got a chance.

"That was rude," he scolded.

"I know. Mom says the same thing about her. She's always flirting with my dad."

The boys returned and pointed to the tidy living room once covered in disarray, cushions, and candy canes. "All done. We're hungry." Both boys looked hopeful.

Chase decided to try his hand at making pancakes and added some of the chocolate chips he knew Tessa always kept on hand. The kids asked for seconds, so he figured he'd done all right. But the mix of carbs, chocolate, and sugar might have been a poor choice for a meal. He could almost see their heads spinning around and their brains creating scenarios a seasoned undercover CIA agent would find chilling.

"I'm going to clean this up then I'll come help you with decorating the living room tree. I see your mom already has a lot done in the family room." The kids carried their plates to the sink. He was a little surprised at first but realized their mom had been raised on a farm and would expect her kids to have chores and responsibilities.

After they hurried into the living room, the sound of plastic tubs being opened soon followed. Remembering he hadn't replaced Tessa's weapon on the top of the china cabinet, he managed to slip in and secure it to a safe position. When he joined them, he noticed how they carefully lifted each decoration to hang it on the tree.

"I wish Mommy was here," Heather sighed as Daniel stroked her hair.

"Me, too," he admitted. "How about some hot chocolate?" Chase wasn't sure if they missed having their mother help, or maybe the evening's adventures had taken a toll on them, but he sensed the need to show a little creative initiation and lighten the mood.

"Mom doesn't usually let us bring food and stuff in here," Sean Patrick announced as he took one of the Santa Claus cups. "But we won't tell, Chase." He smiled over the rim. They sat on the floor, and Chase set the tray holding extra marshmallows and spoons on the coffee table.

Chase narrowed his eyes and met Sean Patrick's hard gaze. "Appreciate it. Maybe I won't tell her about all your shenanigans and potty mouth."

Daniel poked Sean good-naturedly, making him slosh some hot chocolate onto his shirt.

Heather set her cup down and hopped up to continue decorating the tree. She started to sing "Silent Night" as if performing for her part in the church Christmas play. Suddenly, she stopped and whirled around to face the guys.

"What's a virgin, Chase?"

Chase spewed hot chocolate all over the boys' faces. They immediately yelped, and he reached across and frantically wiped at the drips with paper napkins. They grabbed one of Tessa's holiday pillows to mop up the mess.

Once the commotion died down, Sean Patrick grinned at Chase. "Well, aren't you going to answer her question?"

He could never remember a time when a lump formed in his throat because of being tongue-tied or for a lack of words. Yet here he sat with three of the most obnoxious kids on God's green Earth wanting to trap him. How would Tessa handle the question? Why were the boys looking at him expectantly? Were they trying to gain new insight to a grown-up world, or had they been talking with the other boys and looking at dirty pictures? And weren't they too young to be exposed to such things?

Chase cleared his throat and forced down more hot chocolate in the hope the liquid would burn his vocal cords enough to prevent him from speaking. Of all the times for the three to wait patiently like Buddhist monks in meditation... He longed for lots of loud chaos and maybe even a terrorist attack where he could escape to find solace.

Daniel sighed as he turned to Heather. "He probably doesn't know what a virgin is."

Sean Patrick rolled his eyes. "Really? The song is as old as him."

Finally, a moment of distraction descended upon the scene. Chase decided it was a Christmas miracle. "Actually, I know all about the song. Once upon a Christmas Eve, a young priest of St. Nicholas parish church faced disaster. The organ had been pretty much destroyed by mice, and he couldn't afford to get it fixed in time for church services. But the good priest didn't give up."

"What happened?" Heather moved closer to the coffee table and sat down, still holding a string of red beads in her little hand.

The boys leaned in to listen and acted interested.

"He found a poem he had written several years earlier called 'Stille Nacht.' That means quiet night. The priest took his poem to the teacher who played the organ in a nearby town. He asked him to write a melody to accompany the poem on guitar. In several hours, the teacher had the music done, and the carol was played for the first time that night at the Christmas Eve service."

"How long ago are we talking about?" Daniel asked, shoving his glasses farther up on his nose.

"The year was 1818." Chase loved books, especially biographies.

Sean Patrick reached over and patted Heather's hand. "Told you he was old."

Heather's lips pooched out, and her brow creased. "I still don't know what a virgin is, Chasey."

For a second, Chase thought his swallow sounded like a pipe bomb had exploded. Where was a good pipe bomb when you needed it? Her curly head tilted in expectation, and the boys raised their eyebrows in doubt and contempt.

"It's a young lady who hasn't had a baby yet." Chase rushed the words as he dabbed his mouth with a snowflake-printed napkin. He downed the last of the hot chocolate, imitating a gunslinger drinking his last whiskey then gritted his teeth. Maybe he'd answered the question well enough, yet she eyed him. He could imagine the wheels turning in her little female brain. She was a miniature version of her mother, making this day Halloween, not

Christmas.

"Why was her name Ron?"

"Her name wasn't Ron. It was Mary." Chase felt confused. Was this a trap?

Heather sang the song. "Round Ron Virgin, mother and child—" She cut off the song and waited for an answer.

There was no way he couldn't laugh at her interpretation. "It's Round yon mother and child. It means everything around Mary, who was going to have a baby, was calm."

Heather nodded her acceptance and smiled. Chase relaxed and wondered if it would be wrong to pat himself on the back, but he almost choked at her next question. "So, how did the baby get in her belly?"

"I think that is a good question for your mother, since she has had three babies." Did perspiration bead on his forehead? Maybe they should turn off the fireplace.

Sean Patrick landed a friendly blow to Chase's shoulder. "Nice save, Mr. Badass."

Chapter Four

How are things going?" Tessa had decided to call home while she waited for her parents at a coffee shop. She'd already reserved hotel rooms in Reno for them, anxious to be on their way. The crowds of people had slowed, and the arrival and departure boards showed her parents should be landing in the next thirty minutes. They were already two hours later than she'd told Captain Hunter on the last phone call.

"We finished the living room tree. Looks pretty good." Chase sounded calmer this time. She found it difficult to imagine the Delta Force Army captain doing such a normal thing as decorating a Christmas tree.

"Kids doing okay? I know they wanted me to be there to help."

"I think they'll be scarred for life," Chase quipped. "They already show signs of becoming felons."

Tessa smiled at the attempt at humor. "You're just saying that to make me feel better."

"No. I'm serious as a heart attack. Sean Patrick is too big for his britches. Daniel may very well be capable of hacking NORAD and sending us to DEFCON 4. Heather—let's say she's probably going to be the world's best con artist."

"Aww. She is such a sweetie."

"Are you wearing those rose-colored glasses again?" His voice softened the way it did sometimes when they shared a moment of closeness. "I guess they're okay. I think they're plotting even as we speak about how to circumvent my authority. No wonder you eased right into the Enigma team. You've been fighting terrorism for years."

Tessa chuckled and wished she could see the corner of his mouth turn up in a grin. "Have I told you lately you're my hero?"

"Shouldn't your hubby fill that kind of position?" Now, his voice had switched to contempt. He'd never liked Robert and let her know he wondered why she'd married him. They were going through a rough patch and had separated a few weeks earlier, unbeknownst to the kids and her coworkers at Enigma, or so she thought.

"I feel an insult about to be hurled at Robert. If you do, I'm warning you, I'll personally put a lump of coal, not in your stocking but upside your head."

"That's probably what the kids are planning anyway. At least they'd put me out of my misery."

"Chase," she sighed. "I'm sorry."

There was a pause before his warm voice came through the phone again. "I'm yanking your chain. Kids are good. No trouble. I think being a father might not be so bad. This is probably the closest I'll ever get, so thanks."

"Now, you're being too adorable."

He groaned. "Do not ever call me 'adorable' in public, or I'll send your butt back to Afghanistan." When she didn't respond, he continued, "Sorry. I shouldn't have said that."

Tessa hadn't fared well in Afghanistan and still carried the emotional scars of the experience. Chase and her Enigma friends were the only ones in her life who truly understood the turmoil inside her. She'd returned home a different person, and her husband, Robert, had not adjusted to the change.

The twinkling lights of Christmas drew her back to the present, and the smell of her peppermint latte soothed her soul. "What did you get me for Christmas?"

"I'm watching the wild bunch for you. Merry Christmas."

She sighed and almost said I love you but caught herself. "It's what I've always wanted."

"Some little elves want to talk to you. Okay?"

"Sure."

Sean Patrick spoke first and declared all was well. He'd made sure Chase knew the rules even though he wasn't very good at taking orders. She agreed with him and thanked him for his service. He would appreciate the comment. From the time the boy turned five years old, he'd declared he would be going to West Point someday and become a general by the time he was twenty. This always made her laugh. Even now, as he grew older, he hadn't lost the dream, only expanded the timeline a bit. No wonder he and Chase were at odds. Both thought they were in charge.

"I need you to be a good listener, Sean Patrick. Did you know Chase is a captain in the Army?" She could imagine him turning and eyeing Chase with a new kind of respect. "He even went to West Point."

Daniel was soon handed the phone, and he gave a rundown of the evening's events in a logical and orderly fashion. He said Chase might be the best sitter they'd ever had but was kind of old.

"He's a little older than me, Daniel," she corrected.

"My point exactly. I much prefer the cheerleader who lives down the street, but Chase is more fun."

Tessa didn't know when her son had started noticing girls, but he was still a little boy, and that would never do. She wondered what Sean had exposed him to or what website he'd discovered.

"Hi, Mommy." Hearing her daughter's voice warmed her heart. The two of them had a special connection only a mother and daughter shared. "I miss you. When are you coming home? Are Mimi and Poppy with you? Can I talk to them? Where are you? Why aren't you home? Did you know Chase told me all about virgins?"

Her smile faded at the last question. "Slow down. What?"

She repeated all the questions again, only louder. With a deep breath, Tessa tried to remain calm. "I miss you, too. I'll be home tomorrow. Mimi will be here any minute. I'm in Reno, and the snow is blocking the highway, so I have to stay here tonight. Are you being a good girl?"

"Yes. Because I'm a virgin."

"Okay, sweetie. I need you to put Chase back on the phone. Love you." She could hear Heather call Chase to the phone as the boys' remote-control cars sounded like they might have crashed and broken something.

Chase let out an excited "Oh," then laughed. "Set it up again and we'll see how far that puppy will fly." This time his laughter failed to amuse her. "See? We're good."

"What have you been telling my daughter about her being a virgin?"

"The tone in your voice hints you're irritated at me." She could tell he covered the phone for an instant but heard him yell out nonetheless. "No. You can't take the cars outside." Then he turned on the charm. "You were saying? Oh. The virgin thing."

"The virgin thing?" Tessa pulled the phone away from her ear and switched to FaceTime. "Read my expression, Captain Hunter."

Chase tilted his head and grinned at her. "You're missing me?" She started to comment, but he continued. "No. No. Don't tell me." He looked over his shoulder at the kids wrestling in the background then whispered, squinting. "Wondering how to make me a happy man?"

"I know I've said it before, but it is no wonder you aren't married. You are terrible at reading women." He started to speak, but she cut him off. "Don't even say you don't usually do much talking with the brainy bimbos you date. Now. What have you been telling my kids?"

His quick rundown of their earlier conversation caused her to burst into laughter. "Can you even imagine how embarrassed I was?" he admitted. This only made her erupt in laughter again until tears squeezed from the corners of her eyes. "You need to apologize to me," he growled. "Glad to see you're amused." He'd told her many times he loved her laughter. She made life worthwhile in his dark world. When she focused on something other than him, he immediately sounded concerned. "What's wrong?"

"I'm turning the phone around, for you to see this. Recognize her?" Tessa turned the phone toward a woman wearing a backpack, walking down the concourse toward an exit.

"That can't be good."

"I'll follow her."

Chase protested, like she knew he would, so she disconnected the call. Did it turn him into a fuming volcano ready to erupt? Most likely. But she wasn't a novice agent anymore, and the woman she'd encountered years earlier now strolled through the airport. Wherever Honey Lynch showed up, trouble soon followed.

CHAPTER FIVE

The kids stood at the living room window staring out into the night. Something about their quiet demeanor unnerved him. It reminded him a great deal of when he waited for the Taliban to sneak out from behind rocks and out of caves when darkness grew so thick it could be cut with a knife.

The white lights of the decorated tree and the fireplace brightened the room enough for him to evaluate their handiwork. He didn't usually celebrate Christmas. The situation made him consider whether Tessa planned this whole scenario in hopes of giving him a kind of warm and fuzzy feeling. With the children quiet, and the room decorated, he had to admit she knew how to weave magic into Christmas. The house reeked of peppermint bark and sugar cookies.

Growing up in China, his family couldn't celebrate Christmas. Being missionaries in a Communist nation, singing "Oh Come All Ye Faithful" could get you in serious trouble. His parents would quietly tell the story of Bethlehem, baby Jesus, shepherds, wise men, and all the rest, each Christmas. Occasionally he and his sister would get a pair of new socks or a very worn book written in Chinese. Even those had pages missing.

It wasn't until they were sent to Paris to spend Christmas with his grandfather who was serving as the French ambassador that he discovered how people celebrated the holiday in other parts of the world. Those two weeks were eye opening. From there, they traveled to the Qualla Reservation in North Carolina to visit his maternal grandfather. There he got to experience living in a large family with all his Cherokee cousins.

With all the sins he'd committed over the years, Christmas felt like a death trap waiting to make him pay penance for all the pain he'd inflicted in order to keep the country safe. Was this another cruel joke God wanted to play on him? Thoughts of Tessa waiting for her parents at the Reno airport surfaced; another cruel joke God played on him. The woman continued to be a heart attack waiting to happen for him, yet the enticement to be near her remained strong in spite of the do-not-touch zone.

Now he realized even doing an innocent activity like picking up her parents at an airport could get her into trouble. The live feed she sent him was of an Irish assassin named Honey Lynch. She was not supposed to be in the country. The two women had tangled when Honey threatened her family after being put in charge of their care. Tessa never got over the horror and how the woman nearly killed them. There was a chance his junior agent might take it upon herself to hand out a little payback.

Chase pursed his lips after dialing Enigma and left a message about the new development and the current predicament. The sound of muffled laughter alerted him to the prospect of some serious ribbing in the days to follow.

"What are you kids looking at?" Chase asked then slipped the phone inside his vest pocket.

They glanced over their shoulders in synchronized apathy before turning back to stare out the window. The calm and beauty of the room washed a peace over him when he came to stand behind the kids. He spotted activity across the street.

"What is going on over there?"

Several adults dressed in dark clothing appeared to be trying to jimmy the front door while a van waited in the driveway. Another person stood outside the driver's side door and lit a cigarette. The sudden flash of light highlighted a white man, but not much else could be distinguished.

"You know them?"

Sean Patrick frowned back at him. "Mr. and Mrs. Bennett are in

Houston visiting their daughter. We were supposed to keep an eye on their place. They have security—like us."

"How long have they been gone?" Chase bent down and followed their line of sight.

"Brought cookies over three days ago," Sean continued. "Said they were going to have work done on the house when they got back after the New Year. Maybe they decided to have it done while they were gone."

Chase chewed the inside of his lip. Why had he returned Tessa's gun to the hiding spot? He noticed another white minivan several doors down with an exterminator logo on the side. "What about the van? Belong there?" Who killed bugs at night?

"Nope. Their van is red. That's my friend Jose's house. The lights are all on timers, but Jose told me at school they were going to a Christmas movie and dinner tonight. Kind of a tradition for them." Sean squinted and looked up and down the street.

"We used to go with them," Heather confessed.

"How nice," Chase mumbled.

"Guess we won't have any traditions since Daddy moved out," Heather sighed and turned her pretty brown eyes to him with longing.

He straightened like he'd been bee stung. "Moved out?" Did his heart skip a beat? He knew they were having trouble, and had even separated, but he'd thought he was still in the house.

"Mom says things are fine." Daniel reached over and hugged his little sister. "Don't worry. He'll be here for Christmas. You'll see."

"I think I see another van, Chase. Sorry. That is the Martins. They live around the corner. They're teachers, like Mom," Sean Patrick announced, breaking his reverie.

Chase could feel his brow pinch with confusion at this new information about Robert and Tessa's marital situation. He tried to pretend it was of no importance by bending down and forcing himself to assess the ongoing puzzle outside.

"Guess the Bennetts are getting a new TV since that guy is carrying the one to the van." Heather's voice held the same tone of innocence as her mother.

"I think I'll go see what is going on, but I'll call 911 first."

"I'll do it. Hearing a kid's hysterical voice will put the police into motion a little faster." Sean stepped back and grinned.

"We're going to have to have a conversation about your propensity for drama."

Heather joined her brother and nodded. "Yeah. What he said."

"You don't even know what he said." Sean Patrick tugged at one of her curls and laughed.

"Neither do you," she insisted.

"Okay, kids. I'm going over there, and I want you to lock the door behind me. Understand?" All three gathered around him and nodded enthusiastically. "Call 911 and tell them what is going on. I'm going to check things out. Tell them I've gone there so they don't shoot my as—"

"Ass off?" Sean Patrick twisted his lips in a way that made him appear a lot older than ten.

Heather gasped and covered her mouth. "I'm telling Mommy you have a potty mouth."

"Maybe she'll wash your mouth out with soap," Chase suggested with a smirk, liking the image forming in his brain.

Daniel shoved at his glasses on his nose. "Mom is big into timeout."

Chase arched an eyebrow. "Well that explains a lot." He zeroed in on the oldest. "I'm not into timeout, so next time I hear inappropriate language come out of your mouth, I'm going old school on you." He purposely lowered his voice to emphasize each word as if it were a blow to the head. "Got it?"

"Got it." The boy smiled. For whatever reason, Chase wasn't having any luck intimidating this brat, but at the same time he admired his spunk. There was some of his mother showing through him as well.

"You're in charge, tough guy. Lock the door. Call 911. Tell the cops not to shoot me and give them a description. I'll probably be back before they arrive."

"Got it," the children said in unison.

Chase narrowed his eyes, slipped on a cap and coat then pointed to the fireplace. "Turn off the fireplace while I'm gone, and the tree. I don't want any lights on where they'll see you watching. Matter of fact, don't watch. Go to your rooms."

Sean Patrick saluted with two fingers. "Yes, sir." Chase wasn't sure if he was showing respect or mocking him. He could feel his bottom lip jut out in irritation but saluted back nonetheless.

The thought occurred to him as he closed the door and heard the lock snap, he should have called the police himself and let those guys make the collar. Probably the same perps who broke into this house. But that would mean he wasn't in charge, and he didn't know any other way to solve problems.

The snow muffled his approach, but he managed to stay out of the bright spots given off by brilliant light displays in neighboring yards. Normally, his black coat and hat would lend itself to being invisible, but, against the snow, even his dark skin felt like a liability.

He managed to hide behind a tree and watch the uninvited guests of the Bennetts. Strange their security alarm failed, similar to Tessa's. The two men had finished loading the TV and spoke to the driver as he dropped his cigarette in the snow, followed by shoving his bare hands into his coat pockets. All three headed back into the house and flipped on the foyer light after going inside.

This might be the easiest capture he'd ever made. What a bunch of stupid crooks. Even though the snow continued to pile up, Chase remained vigilant to approach with a kind of stealth silence he'd used many times in Afghanistan. You never knew where your enemy might surprise you.

"Looking for something?" came a gravelly voice behind him.

Chase turned nonchalantly and appraised the smoker he'd seen at the van earlier. He'd thought he followed the other two back inside the Bennett house a few minutes ago. This was someone new. Maybe from the white van at Sean's friend's house.

"Yeah. The kids got a Pyrenees puppy for Christmas. Let her out a minute ago, and now I can't find it. Resembles a baby polar bear. Have you seen it?"

The man was shorter than Chase and looked more like the Michelin Tire Man than a threat. Chase cocked his head and smiled, all the while searching for an indication of a pistol bump in the man's coat.

"No. Haven't seen it. You live around here?"

"Hell no. I couldn't afford to live here." Chase smiled. "My sister asked me to babysit the kids while she went to pick our parents up at the airport. She's stuck in Reno," he sighed, "which means I'm stuck with the lollipop kids, if you know what I mean?"

One corner of the man's mouth turned up and nodded. "I'll keep an eye out for the dog."

"Care if I look around for myself? She's pretty shy. I'd hate for her to be out on a night like this. Wouldn't make for a very good Christmas."

The man took a threatening step forward. "Yeah. I mind."

Chase gritted his teeth and smiled. "I thought you might say that."

Before the man could react, Chase grabbed his wrist and twisted so fast, he almost missed hearing the snap. As a scream lifted out of his mouth, Chase rammed him headfirst into the tree, knocking him out. He slid down the trunk face-first.

"Well that is going to hurt in the morning," he mumbled.

CHAPTER SIX

Tessa felt torn. Wait at the gate for her parents or figure out why Honey Lynch had slipped into the country. She watched her look up at the flight boards, exchange glances with a few people around her then meander toward a coffee shop. Chances were good she wouldn't get far. All the roads over the mountains remained closed, and driving anywhere this time of night on slippery roads didn't sound like an option Honey would be willing to chance.

"Excuse me." Tessa located the information center for the airline her parents used when she didn't see them come through the gate. The attendant didn't have good news for her. "I'm sorry. What?"

"Yes. Your parents were delayed in Denver a second time. It was overbooked. They'll take the first flight out in the morning, but it goes to Sacramento."

A groan escaped her throat.

That left finding out what mischief Honey Lynch might be plotting.

Tessa stared down the concourse thronged with holiday travelers. Pushing her way toward the coffee shop, she hoped the Irish assassin was involved in a normal activity, like eating a bear claw and drinking a cup of tea. The idea faded once she stepped inside and scanned the crowd for the redhead.

"Looking for someone?" came a male voice at her elbow.

She glanced down at the man sitting at the table with a to-go cup and a newspaper. Tessa showed him the picture of Honey she'd snapped moments earlier. "Thought I saw my friend come in here. Dressed all in black."

He nodded his shaggy head then took a sip of an iced drink. "Yeah. I think she went into the ladies' restroom," he said, pointing with his cup to the location across from the coffee shop.

"Thanks." Tessa offered a smile.

"Merry Christmas," he countered.

"What?" Tessa felt her eyes narrow.

"Merry Christmas. Feliz Navidad." His white smile almost sparkled on such a light-brown face.

"Oh. Same to you." Tessa moved away, but not before she noticed the white clerical collar.

He spoke again. "Glad I could help!"

Tessa hurried out of the coffee shop and into the restroom. Two elderly ladies hobbled out and smacked into her. With apologies exchanged, she slipped inside. A teenager and her mother argued about her choice of friends as they washed their hands then left. Tessa noticed a cleaning cart outside the restroom and went back to grab the closed sign. She placed the cart and the sign to block the entrance.

The silence gave her pause, knowing being alone with a deadly assassin who tried to kill her once before may have required a plan. This was the exact kind of thing Chase warned her about time after time. Don't go in blind. Have a way out. Expect the unexpected.

Her rubber-soled boots wouldn't give her away as she moved down the row of stalls. Out-of-order signs were taped onto a few doors while a few stood slightly ajar. The one on the end appeared closed.

Standing there with her hands at her side, Tessa slowly reached into her purse to grab her pepper spray. Honey was a crazy, thrill-seeking maniac who got her jollies from being a hired gun for the highest bidder. The name both amused and confused her as she pulled the thumb-size cannister from the hidden pocket of her shoulder purse. Why wasn't her name Vinegar or Sauerkraut? Did she give the name to herself?

"Ahh. A pink pepper spray container," Honey cooed as she

rammed something hard into the middle of Tessa's back. "What will they think of next? Such a cute little thing for a Grass Valley housewife."

Tessa whirled around and raised her hand, but Honey smacked it out away with a gun the size of her palm. She shifted her eyes from Honey to double-check the stall doors.

"Oh. I switched a few of the out-of-order signs." One eye closed and the corner of her mouth tilted up. "I saw you back there talking on the phone. Guess you took my picture and sent it to someone important."

"I did. Captain Hunter."

Her eyebrows lifted, and her lips pooched forward. "So, he's still letting you play secret agent. He must find you amusing." Tessa put on her blank face in hope she showed no fear. "What has our handsome captain been up to lately?"

"Oh, you know. Same old stuff. Kill a terrorist. Save the world. He never tires of it." Tessa dared smirk. Honey took a step closer. "I'm sure he'll be curious as to why you're back in the States. Aren't you on a no-fly watch list?"

Honey smiled big enough her cheeks puffed out. "That I am." The Irish accent sounded thicker than Tessa remembered. "Guess my wit and charm are better than I thought."

For every step Honey took to invade Tessa's space, she'd move two steps back until finally she was up against the wall. In seconds, Honey pushed against her and used her free hand to move Tessa's wayward curl from over her eyes.

Tessa took the opportunity to grab her hand and snap it back so the woman fell to her knees. She found the pressure point on the opposite arm and applied force, releasing the gun into Tessa's hand. But before she could jump away, Honey rolled onto her hip and fanned out her leg to knock her sideways into one of the stalls.

Honey jumped up and plowed toward her. Tessa grabbed the handicap bar and jumped up enough to kick her in the stomach. Unfortunately, Honey grabbed Tessa's foot as she fell against the swinging stall door, pulling her forward in an awkward hop. Tessa realized she'd dropped the gun in the toilet, and Honey now had the pepper spray. To make things worse, the woman could easily snap her leg, leaving her at the assassin's mercy.

There was no love lost between them. The last time she'd seen her had been deep in the bowels of Enigma after her first mission with Captain Hunter. Honey had a professional history with her boss along with a romantic connection. Tessa had wondered about their relationship more than once over the last couple of years.

Honey raised her chin and tightened her grip. Tessa waited for the pain that would drop her, helpless and alone.

"I see you've learned a few tricks since last we met." She shoved Tessa back and released her foot.

Tessa's heart pounded as she tried to catch her breath. Why wasn't Honey in the same physical distress? Maybe because she hadn't had three kids and baked cookies for what felt like the entire town of Grass Valley. Dear God, send an angel to protect me from this maniac, she thought.

"How did you get the gun through security?" Tessa slipped out of the stall to stand before Honey who now reminded her of the cover of a Tomb Raider video. Her skin-tight outfit appeared sinew-strong and deadly.

No wonder Chase Hunter hooked up with her. A fleeting thought of giving herself a gym membership for Christmas faded in and out of her thoughts same as last year at this time. Probably why Agent Samantha Cordova called her Betty Crocker.

"A friend left it in the housekeeping cart outside the facilities. No good to me now since you dropped it in the toilet." She stepped inside the stall and fished it out then tossed it to Tessa who fumbled it midair before managing to get a good grip. Water dripped onto Tessa's boots while Honey moved to the sink to wash her hands.

A hurried passenger rushed into the restroom, searching through her carry-on bag. She lifted her head long enough to see Tessa holding the gun aimed at the Irish assassin. Honey jerked her hands up in surrender and whimpered.

"Please. Don't shoot. I don't have any money."

Tessa spotted the woman and started to explain, but she hightailed it out, nearly dropping her bag.

Honey lowered her hands and nodded toward the door. "I'm out of here. Good luck," she said hustling away. "Follow me, and I'll make you look like a crazed gunman. You'll be dead by the time I reach the front doors." She was almost to the exit when she stopped and turned to smile wickedly. "Be sure to tell your good-looking husband I still think of him on cold nights when the moon is full." She ended with a growl, followed by a laugh.

The thought of Honey Lynch and her soon to be ex-husband, sparked a surge of jealousy she hadn't thought possible. Although she and Robert were having issues, that didn't mean she'd stopped caring for the father of her children.

Tessa ran after her nemesis and managed to drop the gun back in the housekeeping cart. Since she wore her gloves, there wasn't a concern about fingerprints. But as she rushed out into the concourse, she could see security headed her way, along with the terrified woman who had interrupted their confrontation moments earlier. The crowd parted as the woman pointed at the restroom, but a strong arm looped inside Tessa's, and she jerked around to look into gold-flecked eyes.

"Let me help you." It was the reverend from the coffee shop who had identified Honey. "I believe some problems are brewing. Let's stand over here out of the way." He tugged her to stand up against the glass wall of the coffee shop. His voice remained calm and deep. Tessa immediately felt at ease and let him turn to stand in front of her.

The woman and security stopped in front of the restroom. The crowd slowed while others got ushered back or into shops. With guns drawn, they eased into the unknown, leaving the frantic woman to enter the coffee shop and wait.

Tessa feared she'd be recognized, but once again the reverend stepped to her side, blocking a clear view of her face. "Would you like to turn your jacket inside out? I believe it's one of those reversible kinds that are so popular these days."

"What?" Tessa mumbled and glanced down at her red ski jacket. She quickly did as he suggested and slipped the jacket, white side out, into place. "Thanks. I like white better anyway."

He smiled over at her. "Yes. Pure as snow. I also love white. Such an innocent color."

Tessa felt a nervous tickle wash over her but decided she'd become too suspicious over the last few years. This man was a priest, minister, or some religious cleric, so why be afraid? "I probably should go." She sidestepped toward freedom.

The man withdrew long enough to pull on the coat folded across his free arm. "I'll go with you. Your friend seems to have given you the slip. Maybe she, too, went for help." He smiled with the kind of innocence she'd seen in her children when they were trying to avoid getting into trouble.

Security exited the restroom and, while two examined the housekeeping cart, another one talked on his walkie-talkie. They glanced her way then to the woman who had ratted them out.

Tessa slipped her arm back through the reverend's and returned a warm smile. "That would be lovely. Nothing I like better than a guardian angel at Christmas to be an escort."

They moved forward as he laughed out loud. "Then I am pleased to be your escort, Tessa Scott."

She froze and stepped in front of him. "How did you know my name?'

He reached behind her neck and pulled off a sticker. "Says so right here. The sticker says Church of John the Baptist."

"Oh. Sorry. Wore it last week at the live Nativity at our church."

He smiled patiently. "Whew. For a minute I thought you discovered my ability to read minds."

Tessa eyed him before glancing back at security who waved their arms and shouted to get out of the way. One uniformed guard held up the gun by a pencil through the barrel. It soon found its place gingerly into an evidence bag like it might be the baby Jesus. "And here I thought you might be an angel."

"Well, Ms. Scott, Hebrews 13:2 says 'Do not neglect to show hospitality to strangers, for thereby some have entertained angels unawares.' So maybe one of us is indeed an angel."

"Let me put your mind to rest. I'm no angel, and neither is the woman who gave me the slip. I've got to find her."

He patted her hand resting on his forearm. "She isn't far. I'll show you."

Tessa moved along at a leisurely pace so she could steal glances back toward the chaos. "And how do you know that, Reverend—"

"I'm Angelo. You ask a lot of questions, Ms. Scott. I believe there are things you have to take on faith."

"Okay. Now you're talking to the right person."

He beamed a smile her way. "Yes. I know."

CHAPTER SEVEN

‿‿‿‿‿‿‿‿‿‿

With one surprise neutralized, Chase glanced back at Tessa's house to make sure there were no cherub faces watching at the window. He didn't want them to see his violent side. Keeping the kids safe and protected remained a priority. The thought of Heather being afraid of him kept him a little off-balance. This was exactly what her mother did to him every day.

Shouldn't the police be coming into the neighborhood by now? The security gates apparently hadn't stopped these guys. Somebody had the code to open them and drive right in as if they belonged.

He decided the guy he took out was from the van a few doors down and had been waiting for these guys to finish up and help him burglarize the next house. The three remaining burglars exited the house, carrying electronics, a piece of art, and a box of undetermined objects.

"The police are on their way," Chase announced in a calm voice as he approached.

The man with the box staggered backward then dropped his loot, spilling out jars of coins. They fell in the snow with a soft thud but didn't break.

"Get out of our way, buster, or you're liable to get hurt." The shortest man spoke through gritted teeth. His complexion appeared ruddy from the cold; his bulbous nose hinted at a possible drinking problem.

"Yeah, I don't think I'll do that. Who gave you the gate code anyway? I'm impressed you didn't set off the alarm in the house. Did your boss give you the codes when the system was installed? I'm guessing that's how you broke into mine. Didn't figure on someone coming home. I'd be happy to give you a recommendation to whatever clown school you'd like to join after seeing the way you tumbled over the fence." Chase laughed. "That was hilarious."

The three exchanged nervous glances. The two men who still held stolen goods walked to the unmarked van but kept a close eye on Chase. They were probably putting things away to keep them safe until they took care of him—a bigger problem.

"We'll be going now," the chubby guy announced when all three approached him. One held a sledgehammer in his hand, the other two carried crowbars. They meant business. "And you're going to keep your mouth shut, or we might come back and take a look around your house again."

When Chase didn't move, they halted. Bullies weren't used to being stood up to even when they got to be adults. "Since I don't appreciate being threatened, that probably isn't going to work for me. I hate lazy bums stealing from hardworking people." He offered a lopsided grin. "Of course, that's just me."

"You are going to regret ever coming over here," one of the others warned.

"I get that a lot." Chase chuckled, reaching into his pocket. "Who wants to go first?"

All three stepped toward him again like he suspected they would. He held the switchblade close to his side, hidden from their sight, and pushed a button to flip open the blade. It wasn't the first time he'd been outnumbered, but usually they were trained fighters, not knuckleheads with the IQ of a lump of coal.

"Halt!" came a familiar voice.

Chase jerked his head around to see Tessa's three kids dressed in Star Wars costumes. Sean Patrick, the tallest, definitely was Darth Vader, and the other two were nearly invisible, dressed like storm troopers. They held nerf guns created to resemble white machine guns.

"What the hell?" Chase snapped.

"Well looks like you got backup, mister," the leader snorted a kind of laugh.

"Join the dark side," Sean commanded in a deeper voice than Chase thought possible. "It is futile to resist."

Now all three burglars burst into laughter and pointed to the house. "You brats better run along before you get hurt. Wouldn't want you to see what is about to happen to your—"

Immediately, all three kids unloaded their weapons at the men, hitting them square in the face. For some reason, the burglars grabbed at their eyes and hollered like little girls. This gave Chase time to swoop in and give each of them a blow to the head, knocking them to the ground. They rubbed snow on their faces and in their eyes. The knife was returned to his belt before he had to use it.

Sean Patrick took a few zip ties out from under his black robe and handed them to Chase. "Thought you might need these."

Chase snatched them angrily from the boy's hand and proceeded to secure the burglars' hands behind their backs. A police car with lights flashing slid to a stop in front of the house. They exited with guns drawn but quickly returned their weapons to their holsters when they saw the scene had been secured.

"You again," the older policeman declared. He recognized the officer from the church. "You are seeing a lot of action tonight." He cast a suspicious eye toward him as his partner inspected the van before checking the three who had been tied up.

"There's another one over there," Daniel declared. "Chase thumped him pretty good."

The policeman narrowed his eyes at the boy then shifted them to Chase. "Who are you again?"

"He's our babysitter," Heather announced, lifting her storm trooper mask. "He's more fun than most of the ones we've had."

"Was this your idea? Bringing the kids to help you?" The policeman put his hands on his hips and frowned.

Sean Patrick stepped up and lifted the Vader mask. "No, sir. We thought of it on our own."

Chase pinched his nose and shook his head as the three bumbling thieves were jerked to their feet. Tears rolled down their faces, and their eyes were blood red. "What did you put on the nerf darts?" he demanded.

Sean pursed his lips together in a show of resistance. But Heather smiled like an angel, willing to spill the beans. "Mommy has this—"

Daniel covered her mouth with his hand before elbowing his big brother. "Tell him."

"We dipped them in cayenne pepper and onion powder," Sean admitted as he raised his chin in defiance. "You looked like you needed a little help."

The two police officers laughed as they called for assistance.

"You are in a lot of trouble," Chase warned, pointing a finger at the kids one by one.

"But—"

"No buts," he stormed. "You could have been hurt."

"But—"

"Don't interrupt me, Sean Patrick. You should be watching out for your brother and sister," he scolded.

"Well okay. Can't say I didn't try and warn you," Sean Patrick sighed.

Chase got a prickly feeling at the nape of his neck about the same time he heard the cracking of a limb. When he looked up, a pine bough dumped wet snow on his head and down his collar. Laughter erupted not only from the children but the police officers as well. He turned his head toward the kids then slowly removed the snowman appearance from his face.

"Tried to tell you," Sean Patrick smirked.

"Get in the house," Chase ordered. The boys scampered back across the street, but Heather remained. "You, too." He tried to sound cross, but it faded when her little lip jutted out and quivered. He scooped her up into his arms. "What's the matter, sweetheart?"

"Are you mad at us?" she whimpered. "I was scared you were going to get hurt. I didn't mean to be bad. Really."

Chase felt like a heel. "No. No. I'm not mad. I was scared, too." He nodded at the police and told them he'd come in for a statement in the morning. "Let's go home, little angel. Maybe we can make more hot chocolate. Would you like that? I'll even let you help."

"Can I have extra marshmallows?"

"Sure." He carried her across to the house and set her feet on the steps. Instead of hurrying inside, she took his hand and smiled up at him. Now, he really was a goner.

He imagined Tessa like this when she was a little girl. His temper melted away and he felt an unfamiliar warmth rush in his chest when she tugged him toward the door.

"You know you remind me more of Princess Leia than a storm trooper." Chase opened the door for her and bowed.

"My daddy says the same thing," she beamed as she hopped into the foyer.

The mere mention of her father reminded him why he continually circled the fringes of Tessa's life, playing the hero, the advisor, the buddy. It took everything in him not to question the kids about Robert and his possible split from Tessa. If that were true, why hadn't she told him about it? It sounded a lot more serious and permanent than she'd let on.

He double locked the door and turned to observe the three kids sitting on the couch like little angels. Another bad sign. What were they plotting? Or maybe they were remorseful for getting involved across the street. Was it possible they felt guilty he got socked with the wet snow? Then he noticed Sean Patrick arch an eyebrow and realized the kid had only switched to stealth mode.

"I need to dry off," he announced tossing his coat onto a nearby chair. All three kids huddled together and tried to stare at each other to hide their impish grins. With reflection and evaluation of the previous thirty minutes, the whole episode was slightly amusing. He disappeared into the powder room to wipe his face, neck, and hair before leaning against the sink to stare at himself in the mirror.

Creases showed at the corners of his eyes. Rolling his shoulders made stiff muscles ache a little more than they had in a long time. He wasn't getting any younger. Keeping up with three kids made him feel less tough and in shape. At the same time, he felt like he'd never been more alive. What was Robert thinking, screwing up this little slice of heaven? Tessa's image appeared in his mind, causing him to rub a spot over his heart. A heavy sigh escaped from deep inside him as he straightened and decided to see the evening through for her. Maybe he could do something fun with the kids, like a game, or read some books to them.

"You know…" He walked into the living room to find the kids gone. "Hey! Where are you guys?"

Silence.

CHAPTER EIGHT

The airport doors swooshed open, letting a mix of overhead heat and outside cold smack Tessa and her new friend in the face. Snow fell like a Hallmark movie. Parking lot buses pulled to the curb next to the casino ones with an occasional limousine driver assisting high rollers anxious to be on their way.

"I believe she's crossing to the parking garage." Angelo pointed then pulled his coat collar up around a thick neck.

Tessa smiled, even though she didn't take her eyes off Honey. The woman still carried a backpack. She couldn't help but wonder if that, too, had been left for her at the airport and what might it contain. A bomb? A dismantled rifle? What was the intended target?

"Thanks, Reverend—"

"Angelo. Please call me Angelo."

Tessa nodded and waved goodbye as she took awkward steps across the slush to catch up with Honey. Several police cars roared up with flashing lights, along with an unmarked black Cadillac Escalade. She paused long enough to see a familiar face exit the sedan: FBI Special Agent Dennis Martin. He scanned the area until they made eye contact. When his head tilted in recognition and he squinted, she slipped behind a pillar. Why did the FBI show up? Did they know about Honey Lynch being back in the country?

Even though she'd stopped for seconds, the chance of Honey disappearing remained high. She pivoted carefully on the wet surface, afraid it may have frozen. Two rows over, Honey kept pressing her face against the windows of cars. It didn't take a brain surgeon to figure out she planned to steal a car and make an escape.

"The pass over the mountains is closed if you're planning on heading that way." Tessa leaned against a small sedan before shoving her hands into her gloves. She had circled around and made sure she would block another escape.

Honey halted and narrowed her green eyes. With her nose in the air, she took a second to glance behind her. "You are a tad bit stupider than I thought. You know what I do for a living, right?"

"You get paid for not having a conscience." Tessa matched the haughty attitude even though her knees were knocking.

"Well aren't you the little diplomat," she cooed. "Why are you here at the airport?"

"I was supposed to be picking up my parents. They were delayed, and now I can't get home."

"So, you have a car?"

Tessa straightened but remained silent.

"Where is it?"

"First, tell me why you're here. Pretty risky for you. You had to know someone would find out. And for your information, the police are everywhere like ants at a picnic."

Honey's mouth turned up at one corner. "Cute. They aren't looking for me. No way they know where I am."

"Who is your target?"

"My target?" she snapped. "I don't hurt anyone who doesn't deserve it. You'd best be happy about that, or your handsome husband would be dead. Sometimes I merely watch and make suggestions. This time, I'm trying to warn a friend."

"Ever hear of the phone? How about the Internet?" Tessa huffed.

"Couldn't take a chance on being traced or followed. I thought if I got here first, I would be ahead of the game. Maybe lend a hand."

"You're talking riddles," Tessa accused. "Just tell me. I won't turn you in." Honey started to walk off but Tessa rushed to cut her off. "Who. Is. The. Target?"

"Captain Chase Hunter," she snarled.

Tessa tried to speak and couldn't help but stagger backward. "Why?"

"He's made a lot of enemies. I'm trying to warn him. If I get to him in time—"

"No. That can't be."

"Such a silly woman," Honey spat. "It is a preemptive strike. An old enemy decided to eliminate him before he caught onto what he's up to."

"This can't be happening." She put her palms on both sides of her face. "Come on. My car is over here."

Tessa tried to turn away, but Honey reached out and jerked her around. "Why are you going to help me?"

"Because Chase is babysitting my kids."

Honey paled. "Holy Mother of God."

The SUV was located in short order, but the cars parked on each side of it had pulled in so close the women couldn't even open the doors. Tessa clicked the rear lock and opened the hatch.

"I'll crawl in. Give me the keys, and I'll back it out." Honey held out her hand. "Well, come on," she demanded. "We don't have all day."

"How do I know you won't drive off without me?" Tessa's scowl furrowed her brow.

"Ya don't know, so you best be trustin' me, 'cause I don't think ya have a choice." She snatched the keys and shimmied up into the back, shoving aside the backpack she carried for emergencies and several blankets, to crawl over the seats.

The woman appeared to be a virtual monkey and managed to slip behind the wheel and start the ignition in no time. Tessa had decided to crawl in after her when Honey yelled to shut the hatch. She hesitated for only a second before following instructions then stepped aside right before Honey got a little too close to the car on the passenger side, taking off the side mirror of both cars.

She picked up momentum after the ripping sound and turned the car toward the exit. Tessa ran up to the passenger side. When she grabbed the door handle, Honey inched forward and leveled a condescending glare her way. The cat-and-mouse game continued for several more minutes until Tessa halted and slammed her palm against the window.

"Stop the freakin' car, you crazy sociopath," she screamed.

Honey powered the window down and frowned. "I'm not crazy."

Jerking the door open, Tessa spit out, "That is debatable." She slid into the seat.

~ ~ ~ ~

Silence from three kids meant the real possibility of a nuclear meltdown. Life as Chase knew it would soon be over if he didn't locate and intercept a possible first strike. The sooner he neutralized the problem, the sooner the risk of being tortured and killed by their mother would be drastically reduced.

"I'm going to find you," he called out in his Delta Force voice. "And when I do, you'll pay for making me search for you."

Silence.

The lights were now out in the kitchen and adjoining family room. He inwardly moaned—of all times not to be carrying night vision goggles. Maybe, if he ever became a father, such things should be added to the gift registry. That was equipment every parent would eventually find useful.

He grabbed an empty three-foot cardboard wrapping-paper tube to have at his side in case of an attack. And there would be an attack.

When his eyes adjusted to the dark, he spotted them kneeling behind a cushioned bench used as an ottoman. An unidentifiable object sat atop it. He couldn't make it out until, at the click of a lever, something hurtled toward him. He dodged at supersonic speed but overcorrected and took a bean bag to the eye. The projectile dropped into his hand when he shut the targeted eye, only to be hit again.

Chase dropped onto his back, paralyzed with the knowledge another attack would be coming. Small voices whispered with excitement as they crept closer. When they leaned over him, Chase sprang up with a hellish roar, causing all three kids to scream and fall in various clown-like positions. He swung out his carboard tube and twirled it like a Samurai sword.

The boys bounced up onto the couch with their own carboard

swords pulled back to imitate the rebel forces he knew them to be. Chase twirled his sword one more time before dropping a disgruntled glare on Heather, who appeared to be without a cardboard weapon.

She batted her eyes, reminding him of her mother doing the same thing in times of stress. Her cherub voice broke the silence as she fanned out her hands in a new kind of plea from the iconic Star Wars princess, Leia Organa. "Help me, Obi-Wan Kenobi. You're my only hope."

Sean Patrick, aka Darth Vader, lowered his mask and growled at his little sister, "I find your lack of faith—disturbing."

Both boys jumped from their positions and swung their weapons, making contact with their counterparts. A certain amount of grunting and garbled threats came with each swipe of the sword. Chase didn't hold back when he smacked Sean Patrick upside the head then on the back of the knees as he tried to deflect another blow. Daniel was gaining on his sister with each swing, forcing her to walk backward.

"Obi-Wan," she called frantically.

Chase managed to shove Sean Patrick back down on the couch by using the end of his sword against his chest. He stormed toward Daniel and whacked him on top of the head; that got his attention. With a wobbly pivot toward him, Daniel made contact with the side of Chase's face. It surprised him enough that he didn't notice the approaching danger until something heavy launched onto his back.

The combined force of Daniel's blows to his side and Sean's choke hold helped the ex-Delta Force captain to realize he'd met his match. He lost his footing when his legs hit the side of the couch. Sean backed off, bouncing onto the floor.

"Now, Daniel!" he yelled.

The next thing Chase knew, Daniel lunged at him, knocking him over the arm of the couch, onto the couch cushions for only a second then he slid to the floor into a lopsided sitting position. He held up his hands in laughing surrender. All three kids jumped on him with affectionate hugs and uncontrolled giggles. Soon they were all panting with exhaustion and trying to stand, only to have Chase try to knock their feet out from under them.

Daniel did manage to switch to a Yoda voice to declare, "The

Force is strong with this one, Sean Patrick." More laughter filled the room until everyone held their sides.

"Okay. Enough," Chase said rolling to his knees then stood. "I think I hear my phone." He felt his pocket. "Where's my phone?" The kids cocked their heads, listening for the sound while lifting cushions and peeking under the couch.

"Found it." Sean held it up. Before Chase could rescue it, the oldest answered the ring. "Mom! Guess what? We beat the crap out of Chase. It was so much fun."

"Give me that." He snatched the device out of the kid's hand and shoved him gently away by placing his palm on his forehead. "Hello. Tess?" The phone started to cut out, but she sounded alarmed. Had she followed Honey? Maybe something had gone wrong with her parents?

"Chase, what is going on?"

"I'm fine. We were horse-playing. Did your folks make it?"

"No. They didn't. Now listen to me." Tessa talked faster, making him question if he heard her correctly. Why was she so upset? "There's a problem."

"Stay as long as you need. We're good." He grinned at the kids. "Right, guys?" They cheered, flipping on lights and throwing Christmas pillows at him.

"Will you shut up?" she stormed. "You're in danger."

"I know." He jumped when one of the kids shot him in the butt with a nerf gun bullet. "Knock it off," he warned. "Sit down until I get off the phone," he ordered. "I may be wrapped in duct tape by the time you get back."

"Chase." His body stiffened at an Irish accent. "Tessa is trying to tell you an assassin is coming for you. They may already be in Grass Valley."

"Do you know who?"

The static prevented him from understanding anything else for a few seconds. "Get. Safe place. Dead…" Then the line cut off.

CHAPTER NINE

Chase lowered the bamboo shades in the family room then moved to the other downstairs rooms. Unfortunately, most of the windows were draped in sheers or nothing but a thin woven shade. Tessa decorated like she was still living on a farm in rural Tennessee and everyone in the area possessed an abundance of Southern hospitality and charm. He checked the locks on the doors and windows followed by turning off lights.

"We're hungry," Heather announced.

"I just fed you. Isn't it getting close to your bedtime?" Chase turned on the outside floodlights.

"No. There's no school tomorrow, so Mommy said we could stay up later."

Daniel and Sean Patrick entered, sucking on Fudgsicles.

"Does your mother let you walk around with ice cream?" Chase's brow furrowed, and his left eye twitched.

Sean Patrick blinked as he ran his tongue around the outside of his chocolate-coated mouth. "Technically, this isn't ice cream. So, I guess we're good."

Daniel dropped his on the floor and bent to pick it up when Sean Patrick bumped him with his hip, sending him flat on the floor, squishing the Fudgsicle in two different directions. To Chase's surprise, the boy jumped up and rammed his head into

Sean Patrick's stomach, sending the other Fudgsicle flying into Heather's hair.

The little girl opened her mouth and let out a wail that could wake the dead. Both boys continued to take punches until Chase reached over and picked them up, one under each arm. He carried them to the family room and dropped them on the couch.

"Stay," he barked then returned to a crying Heather.

He kneeled and tried to remove the remaining Fudgsicle from her hair. It slid down her face before he could catch it, leaving a chocolate trail.

"Come on, sweetness," he coaxed as he stood and took her hand. "Let's get you cleaned up."

He led her to the kitchen, casting a quick glance at the boys who he guessed landed a few more blows in his absence based on their quick attempt at sitting still and placing their hands in their laps.

Setting Heather up on the counter, he wet a clean cloth to wash her face and hands. The hair was a little trickier, but she stopped the crying and stared at him with her round eyes. Chase decided having little girls instead of boys was a lot easier to deal with on a physical plain. Emotionally, that was up for debate. Females could be so dramatic.

"There. All better. Pretty as a peach again," he declared. But her bottom lip jutted out, and the eyelashes batted a warning of returning tears. He saw a bowl of colored candy canes and offered her one. "Happy?"

She shook her head even as he helped her unwrap the candy. "Will you play with me?"

"Sure. What do you want to play?" He took a towel and tried to dry the curls he'd soaked moments earlier.

"Princess school."

The sound of the new activity troubled Chase, especially when he heard the boys snigger. "I don't know how to play princess school. Maybe we could play a card game or—"

Heather beamed. "I'll teach you, Chasey." Her excitement spilled over into clapping her hands.

He rolled his eyes up to the ceiling and rethought the idea girls were easier. "Well, first, why don't we knight those two in there, and we can build a fortress to protect our castle. We want to make sure if any rough characters, I mean evil empire types, come calling, we are ready. Your mother seems to think we need to take precautions in case any more bad guys come around tonight. Probably a good idea. What do you think?"

The boys hurried into the kitchen, arms wrapped around each other's shoulders. All was apparently forgiven between the two. Heather, on the other hand continued to have a pouty mouth and folded her little arms across her chest, reminding him once more she was a carbon copy of her mother. Yep. Boys were much easier.

"I got a few ideas, Chase," Sean Patrick announced with enthusiasm.

Chase's jaw tightened, his eyebrow arched at the prospect of the oldest being in charge of future troops on the front lines. "I bet you do."

Daniel rubbed his chin like a wise old man. "I think I can set something up with the outside cameras."

"Outside cameras?" Chase hadn't heard about Tessa having those.

"Daddy wanted Mommy to put them in so she could see when the USP man came with Amzon boxes." Heather bobbed her head, presenting this new information.

"Or if porch pirates tried to steal them," Daniel interjected while swinging an imaginary sword. "And it isn't USP, or Amzon, Heather."

She raised her nose and sniffed. "Mommy thinks it's cute when I say that."

Chase lifted her off the counter and set her feet on the floor. "Yeah. It is kind of cute, but you are going to have to be the princess in charge, so cute ain't gonna cut it, Your Majesty." He handed her a rolling pin from Tessa's collection on the counter. "This is your scepter and weapon." Next, he tried to sound dramatic, imitating a character from one of his favorite Indiana Jones movies. "Use it wisely." He bowed his head and placed a fist over his heart. The boys quickly followed suit.

Heather jumped up and down. "This is going to be fun," she squealed.

"I doubt that," Chase mumbled.

~ ~ ~ ~

Tessa checked her watch as Honey pulled out onto the highway. It was past bedtime for the kids, she thought. Maybe Chase could concentrate on protecting her family once the children were asleep. Cell phones weren't working, thanks to the storm over the mountains, and roads were closed until the plows could clear them. As long as it kept snowing, that would be impossible. The weather forecast, according to the radio, predicted clearing skies after midnight. The trucks would need another couple of hours to work their magic then maybe they'd be able to head to Grass Valley.

"Can't we call the Highway Patrol to contact Grass Valley P.D.?" Honey asked as she pulled into the parking lot of the Lucky Lady Hotel and Casino. "This was where you were bringin' your mum?"

"We can try, but I'm not sure they're going to believe us and might just hang up. Even worse, they might take down the info and put us on a list of crazy people. People in ditches, or accidents and diverting traffic is the priority." Tessa unbuckled and took a closer look at the area. "Oh. This looks fancy and out of my price range. Mom and Dad would love it though. It was the first place I called that said they had a vacancy. Christmas. Don't people stay home anymore?"

"According to the sign, it has the largest burlesque show in Nevada. Your mum into that?"

"Don't get all high and mighty on me, Honey. You're no Girl Scout."

"I am when it comes to my mum," she admitted opening the door. "Let's get something to eat. Maybe we can figure this out." Tessa continued to sit in the car and stare out the windshield. Honey walked around, opened the door, and bent down to peer in. "Have you ever known Captain Hunter to not be in complete control of a situation once he knew trouble was headed his way?"

Tessa turned to stare at the woman she'd once despised. "But my kids…"

"Come on with ya," she said, laying a hand on her shoulder. "Chase isn't going to let anything happen to those wee ones. Besides, we may still be able to stop this ourselves." She stepped back as Tessa eased out of the car.

"What do you mean?"

"Buy me dinner, and I'll tell you." Honey left her standing there until Tessa decided to catch up and play along. Honey reached over and pinched her cheek and laughed. "That's a good girl."

Tessa jerked away and added a shove to the woman's shoulder. "Don't touch me."

"That isn't what your husband said when I did the same to him," she taunted.

Tessa let loose a growl then stuck out her foot, tripping the assassin so she fell face-first in the snow. She smiled with satisfaction as the woman raised herself to her knees. "Oops. My bad."

With a feeling of satisfaction and victory, Tessa moved away toward the path leading to the hotel. A banshee yell came from behind her and, before she could twist around, something hit her from behind, knocking her to the ground. Honey straddled her and proceeded to rub her face in the fresh powder.

"How do you like that, you pathetic little housewife?" Honey laughed as she rolled off and to her feet. Tessa eased up but slipped and fell butt first in the snow. When Honey extended her hand to assist, she slapped it away and managed to stand on her own.

"Don't ever mention my husband again, or I'll show you what this housewife is really made of."

Honey grinned from ear to ear. "I think I'm going to like you after all, Tessa Scott."

"Well, the feeling isn't mutual."

Honey made kissing sounds toward her. "Not yet. I grow on people."

"So does a wart. Doesn't mean I want one."

Honey came up beside her, put her arm around her neck, and squeezed lightly, even as Tessa tried to shove her away. The assassin only laughed until she'd had her fun then released her as they walked through the front door.

~ ~ ~ ~

"Carol of the Bells" played in the hotel lobby decked in sparkly colored lights and garland. The smell of warm sugar cookies had been pumped into the air, layering another artificial experience to Christmas. He saw the two women bickering as they headed toward the casino, while he held the door for an elderly couple.

Following Honey Lynch proved to be more labor intensive than he'd first believed when he took the job. After the leak finally made it to her ears about taking out Captain Hunter, he was contacted to clean up the loose end. A little extra spending money at Christmas would be well worth the effort and the paycheck. Part of him wanted to see where this scenario led.

He knew Hunter and even admired him. The Irish pain-in-the-neck carried an impressive resume, but they had never crossed paths. She'd taken out a friend's brother years ago then disappeared. Now here she was, in the crosshairs of revenge. Would it be worth the money? He certainly didn't want to get on Hunter's bad side.

Hunter didn't concern him as much as the powerful man holding his current paycheck though. The guy apparently wanted the situation dealt with before stepping onto the world stage with his next new venture. The only information he'd received about Captain Hunter was he could be dangerous if provoked, but he already knew that. Other than working at a university and in the Army reserves, Hunter wasn't easy to intimidate. Since the captain and Honey Lynch were friends, he needed to be governed by a sense of caution. The captain had an unwavering loyalty to friends and would break the law to help them in a pinch.

Whoever this Tessa Scott might be, she didn't appear to be on friendly terms with the Irish witch. Watching them roll around in the snow had amused him enough to stay for the show. He'd spotted them in the parking garage earlier, and, even then, their engagement was laced with conflict. Nothing like a female cat fight to get him all worked up. He wondered if he'd be able to take advantage of the discord for his own physical pleasure along the way. It had been a while since he'd taken the time to enjoy himself.

Everything would have gone smoothly if it hadn't been for Special Agent Dennis Martin showing up at the airport with an FBI entourage. Those government storm troopers had messed up his party more than once. How did he find out he was in Reno? And why, when he saw Tessa Scott, did he go after her? No matter. It gave him the time to escape undetected. Knowing the FBI's propensity for investigation, it would only be a matter of time before he located her, if, in fact, that was his goal. Maybe he could still get away with the money he'd stolen.

For now, he'd wait. Watch. Plot. Access. Follow. Then do his job.

CHAPTER TEN

Chase eyed the children with a new kind of concern. Knowing Honey Lynch took it upon herself to warn him of trouble meant not only was he in danger, but these kids were as well. Honey knew and worked for a number of unsavory people, but, in recent years, she'd appeared to have developed a conscience. There were jobs she refused to take anymore, no matter the dollar amount. Tessa's husband was proof the woman could change her mind on carrying out a hit. Robert never knew how close he and the children had come to being a fulfilled contract.

Now Tessa, apparently, had teamed up with the woman she despised and trusted about as much as a black mamba. They'd tangled once before when Tessa discovered the assassin watched over her family. Only Chase's reassurances and half-truths, promising Honey would watch after them, calmed her down enough to follow him into danger. Both women were nearly killed in the end. Ah. The good old days when he didn't have women to mess up his orderly world. At times he thought fighting in Afghanistan was a walk in the park compared to his life with Tessa Scott the last few years.

Now, neither of the women had him to moderate their unpredictable personalities and anger issues. One had an overabundance of guilt and conscience and the other had no conscience and regretted nothing she did. These days, distinguishing between the two women became increasingly more difficult.

"What ya thinkin' about, Chasey? Are we playing princess school or not?" Heather's sing-song voice brought him back to reality.

"Of course. However, I think I heard the kingdom is in danger and we need to protect the castle."

The boys straightened to their full height and puffed out their chests.

"Tell us what to do, Sir Silent Knight," Sean Patrick demanded with a deeper voice.

"Sir Silent Knight?"

"Well, you're the one who knows so much about the song," Daniel said.

Chase eyed the boys like he often did a captured insurgent, the difference being these boys didn't blink. Not a good sign. How did Tessa juggle being a mom, Enigma agent, professor at the university, and a wife of a self-centered lawyer? Did she possess superpowers he wasn't aware of? Maybe this was true of most women, and he'd never been with one long enough to find out.

"Silent Knight it is, then," Chase said. "Let's make a plan for a few traps. Sound like fun?"

Their bobbing heads and Heather's enthusiastic clapping indicated he'd hit a home run. If push came to shove, he wanted to know the kids would be safe and unharmed. If they were in for a visit from one of his enemies, he wanted to make sure he could neutralize the danger without exposing the kids to the harsh realities of what he and their mother did for a living.

~ ~ ~ ~

"You're out of your mind." Tessa pushed away the carrot cake Honey ordered for them to split. The other woman quickly pulled it closer and proceeded to finish it off. "How can you be so skinny and eat like a Marine?"

Honey took the last bite and moaned with delight. "My job burns up a lot of energy."

"Speaking of burn—at least you'll be used to it when you go to

Hell."

She pointed her fork like a gun. "Now that hurt. I'm a good Catholic girl. I'm covered in that department."

"Did you miss the lesson on thou shalt not kill? Because I'm pretty sure to be a good Catholic you can't have assassin as a job description."

"It's in the fine print." She smiled. "Besides, I go to confession whenever I can."

"Do you always make things up as you go along?"

Honey scraped the remaining icing onto her fork then slowly licked it from the prongs. "Usually, I have a backup plan for the plan. I didn't count on you or your wee ones getting in the middle of this. So, I'm trying to think. Eating helps me think."

"Based on the amount of short ribs and fries you inhaled, I'm expecting something to put the Navy SEALs to shame. What you just told me makes no sense at all."

"Okay. Maybe I was thinking through my hunger issues. I'm clearheaded now." She leaned back in her chair and surveyed the other patrons. "I bet between the two of us we could get a lonely Romeo to take us over the mountains to Grass Valley."

Tessa covered her face with her palms while shaking her head. "Oh, that is a much better plan!"

A man approached their table. "We meet again, Ms. Scott. I see you found your friend."

Tessa smiled. "Reverend Angelo. What a surprise." She hoped the obnoxious smirk on Honey's face wouldn't be followed by some disrespectful comment. "Yes. This is my friend, Honey Lynch."

The assassin jutted her hand out like it might really be a dangerous sword and grabbed his hand. "Angelo. Italian for Messenger of God. Appropriate." She continued to hold his hand.

Tessa noticed the two locked eyes and appeared to be evaluating each other. The good reverend even tilted his head and narrowed his eyes. How many times had she seen Chase do that before…?

"Nice to meet you, Ms. Lynch." He managed to pull his hand away.

"So, are you the good kind of messenger from God or the kind who throws sinners into the pits of Hell?"

"Honey!" Tessa growled. "Can you be any more inappropriate?"

Honey offered a thin smile toward her then stood. "Excuse me. I need to use the ladies' room."

"Please, Reverend Angelo, have a seat. I apologize for my—for Honey. She can be blunt and a little unfiltered."

He pulled out a chair to face the direction Honey disappeared. When he shifted his eyes to Tessa, a wave of uncertainty washed over her. Most pastors she'd known weren't as muscular as Angelo. She hadn't noticed earlier the scar above his clerical collar or how his hands, now folded on the table, were calloused and tanned. When she dared return her gaze to meet his, she found him staring at her with dark, hooded eyes. They reminded her of a vampire.

"You don't look like a priest or pastor."

"You don't look like the kind of woman who pals around with an assassin, either."

Tessa jumped up, but Angelo grabbed her hand before she could slip away.

"Who are you?"

A slow smile spread across his narrow lips. "Sit down, Mrs. Scott."

~ ~ ~ ~

Chase wondered again if he should call someone to come get the children. The neighbors were gone or they'd would be watching them for Tessa. The rest of the team were in Sacramento or on leave. Besides, getting to Grass Valley would take at least an hour in this weather. There was the cougar lady, but that seemed to pose other problems. If he tried to make a run for it, whoever was after him might be waiting to make a move. He could also have an accident on the slick roads, leaving them sitting ducks. Better to hunker down and prepare for the worst.

"We got some good stuff, Chase," Sean Patrick, a soldier in the making, declared.

He watched the kids spread their ideas onto the table. A jar of mixed buttons. One bag of marbles in assorted sizes. A game of jacks still in an unopened package. Three slingshots and two water guns. He picked up the game of jacks.

Daniel explained, "Not sure what jacks are. My grandma said she used to play with them when she was a kid, and we should learn how to play, too. Dad never let us open them. Said we'd leave them on the floor to step on."

Next, he fingered the slingshots. "Uncle Jake got us those."

Chase remembered meeting the old coot, Uncle Jake, after a near disastrous encounter. He was tough and dangerous. "Does your mother let you play with these?"

"Only when we're supervised." Sean Patrick grinned.

"I'm guessing you boys practice unsupervised when she's not around."

The boys eyed him. "You aren't going to rat us out, are you, Chase?" Daniel asked.

"No. Can you hit a target?"

"Nine times out of ten for me, and Daniel is almost as good."

Chase looked at Heather, who snuggled her stuffed unicorn. "What about you? Can you use one of these slingshots?"

"Mommy says I'm too little. I might put an eye out."

"Smart Mommy." He patted her unicorn's head then handed her the package of jacks.

Most likely, whoever showed up would be carrying guns. How would he manage to disarm them without anyone getting hurt? Exposing the kids to gunfire and dangerous men was not a scenario he'd ever had to work through.

Now here they were, looking at him like he'd asked them to design a new ride at Disneyland. Their wide eyes and innocent grins touched him in a place he never knew existed. They were part of the same magic spell their mother continued to throw at him each time she walked into a room. These feelings of tenderness, fear, and helplessness annoyed him. How was he supposed to anticipate the unexpected with unicorns and slingshots mudding up the waters of reason?

"Okay, knights—"

"I'd rather be a Jedi if you don't mind," Daniel said.

"Okay. Jedi it is."

"Not me. I think I'd like to be a plain old badass like you." Sean Patrick's eyebrow rose slightly as he tilted his head.

"I'm telling Mommy you have been cussing all night." Heather pointed her unicorn at her brother.

One corner of his mouth twisted up as his eyes darted from Heather to Chase. "Women."

"I hear ya," Chase said offering him his fist so they could bump knuckles. "One Jedi and one badass." Heather lowered her head and pooched out her lips. She looked up through her bangs at him, resembling a disgruntled chipmunk. He squatted and tickled her cheek until she smiled. "You are the bravest princess I've ever known to stand up to these two characters." And, instantly, her temper dissolved. She grabbed him around the neck and squeezed.

"You are really Mr. Tootsie Roll Pop, Chasey."

Chase pushed her hair out of her face and couldn't help but grin at the cherub face. "I am? How so?"

"You are hard on the outside but soft on the inside."

Chase sighed and rubbed his face in exasperation to hide the possibility she was getting to him. "That has to be the cutest thing I've ever heard. But it isn't very scary. I think I'll stick with Silent Knight."

"Okay, kids. This is what we're going to do."

~ ~ ~ ~

Tessa sank back into her chair and took a moment to survey the people milling about the restaurant before turning her attention back to Angelo.

"Who are you? I mean really."

"I'm Angelo. Truth."

"A messenger from God."

"Believe what you want." Angelo spoke in a more sinister manner than when they'd met in the airport. "You don't have anything to worry about, Tessa. I mean you no harm."

"Where have I heard that before?"

"Captain Hunter, I'm guessing." He offered a sly grin.

"How do you know him? What is going on?"

"You tell me. You're the one hanging out with a known terrorist."

"We're trying to get to my house. Captain Hunter is watching my children tonight, and they are in danger."

"I see. That might be why your face is as white as your jacket."

He stood and touched her chair, signaling she should also stand. "We should go."

"You haven't answered my question, and I'm waiting for Honey."

"She left the restaurant when I joined you. She's a tricky one."

Tessa pulled on her coat and fumbled for a credit card to pay the bill when a waiter came to clear the table.

"No charge. The bill has been paid."

She swallowed hard. "Honey doesn't have any money."

"She does now. She stole your credit card. Let me help you." He laid a hand on her back. "Trust me."

CHAPTER ELEVEN

❦

Tessa stepped out of Angelo's touch on her back. "I'm sure she is outside. Patience isn't her strong suit. Besides, I have the car keys." Unconcerned, she reached in her purse to the pocket where she always stored her keys.

"Everything all right?" Angelo asked as she started a frantic dig into the abyss of her purse.

"Can't find my keys." She dumped the contents on the crumpled napkin then explored the interior of the purse one more time. Next came the pat down of her pockets, followed by looking under the chair and table. "I don't understand."

Angelo lowered his head and stared up with a sinister smirk. "I think you do."

"Honey? She even stole my car keys?" Tessa took a deep breath and growled a response. "Since my phone is also missing, I'm guessing she took that, too." Throwing her hands in the air, she surveyed the restaurant and out into the casino area. "It was a huge mistake trusting her."

"I have a car." He pulled out a phone and handed it to her.

Tessa stared at the offering and felt a temptation to snatch it away from him. However, she really didn't want her home phone or Chase's cell phone number to be in this guy's dialing history. Calling her husband was a waste of time since he remained stranded at O'Hare Airport in Chicago.

Her fingers began to fidget, and her heartbeat increased. Suddenly, the down jacket felt too hot and tight. She needed some fresh air. Shoving all the stuff she'd dumped on the table back into her purse, Tessa zipped it shut then turned to say goodbye to the mysterious man of God or whatever he pretended to be. But he was nowhere to be found.

Once outside, she concentrated on getting her bearings even as the snow fell faster. Should she walk out into a parking lot all alone at this time of night to find her car? Chances were good Honey had made her escape without so much as a second thought about leaving her behind. She probably thought it impossible she might search for her in a creepy parking lot where priest impersonators and other boogeymen lurked.

Outdoor speakers piped "White Christmas" loud enough that arriving guests raised their voices to talk to the valets, causing Tessa to feel another layer of chaos. After slipping her backpack purse into place, she dropped her hands to her side and inhaled the smell of freshly fallen snow.

"It's going to be all right. It's going to be all right," she mumbled. It felt like she'd changed the words "There's no place like home" in The Wizard of Oz. Instead of a scarecrow and a tinman, she had an Irish assassin and a questionable priest. That Dorothy chick had all the luck. "I can do this."

"Do what?" It was Honey.

Tessa felt torn between gathering her in her arms for a hug and slapping the smug expression off her face.

"Where have you been?"

"The ladies' room. Are you deaf? What's the deal leaving me?"

"I thought, I mean, Father Angelo said you, I…"

"Father Angelo, my aunt Kathleen's caboose," Honey growled. "If he was a priest, then I'm the Virgin Mary." She crossed herself, kissed her fingers, and lifted them to Heaven. "Forgive me, Lord Jesus."

Tessa exhaled so hard it moved the bangs covering her eyes. "Oh brother. Forgive you? Talk about a full-time job. No wonder things aren't getting done for the rest of us. You're a piece of work. You know that?"

Honey smirked and started toward the parking lot. "Of course I do, but it warms my heart, knowing you see it, too."

"I meant because you took my credit card and my keys. The only reason you aren't gone is because I was on my way out here to try and stop you." Tessa trailed after the woman, slipping and sliding as she tried to keep up. She wondered why Honey could walk across the frozen surface like she might be strolling down a runway in Paris during fashion week.

The assassin stopped in the middle of the central driveway, causing a car to slide around her, and the driver laid on the horn. Tessa grabbed her elbow and towed her into the first parking lot.

"I donna know what you're talking about. I didn't take your keys or card. So are ya telling me we can't get out of here?"

"But Father Angelo said—"

"Back to him. He was playing you." She pointed to a line of cars. "Should be over there." Amazingly, the car remained exactly where they'd left it. "A freakin' Christmas miracle it's still here with you believing that smooth talker."

Tessa found the key she'd hidden in the wheel well. Both women quickly got in the car.

"No. No. No." Tessa pounded the steering wheel. "A key has been jammed into the ignition and bent. And it isn't mine. Whoever took my key ring also has my house key and office key."

"Probably your priest again. Don't you have one of those cars you start up with your voice or something? Or maybe Enigma can start it remotely." She reached over and tried to remove the key.

"This is an old car. Enigma wants me to upgrade, but my husband didn't think I needed a new car. Instead, he bought one for himself. 'All about the image,' he said."

"The image I'm getting of Robert is with a pitchfork stuck through his selfish heart. I mean, with you having the wee ones and all. He should be ashamed."

Her voice sounded so matter-of-fact and calm, Tessa couldn't help but stare at her before speaking. "I think that is the nicest thing you've ever said to me."

She opened the car door and pushed out. "I kinda grow on people."

"Like a wart." Tessa followed the woman's example.

"You're a funny one. Does Enigma keep you around for comic relief, or are you mostly used as bait?"

Tessa wondered about the same thing at times, considering they were the president's special team of misfits who did things the CIA and FBI couldn't do because of the law.

"They keep me around for my keen eye and intuitive nature."

Honey halted long enough so she could bend over laughing. When she stopped, a tear rolled down her face. She wiped it away and finished with another half laugh.

"I got news for you, Miss Domestic Wonder Woman. You are around to keep the high and mighty Chase Hunter from going off the deep end. He's one national security incident away from taking the law into his own hands. You're the one thing keeping him on the straight and narrow." The assassin started looking in car windows. Tessa figured she was about to steal her first car.

"That is ridiculous. We're friends. Why does everyone keep thinking there is romance going on between us? I'm sick of it. Enigma needs me and not because I have Chase on a short leash."

Honey stopped suddenly and whirled around, causing Tessa to crash into her. A devious smile turned up one corner of her mouth.

"You are adorable."

Tessa's face heated up with a flare of temper. She didn't want to be treated like a mascot for a bunch of sketchy Enigma agents. The thought had occurred to her more than once that she'd become a living, breathing dose of a strong antidepressant for the group. She'd been told on more than one occasion she was their conscience. They even called her their "good girl."

"Our chariot awaits, Cinderella." Honey placed her hand on the door handle of the Cadillac Escalade and opened it. "Hop in. I'll get this running in no time."

"Honey, I think this car belongs to the FBI. Look at the license plate!"

She slid in and explored for a set of keys. When she found a keyring under the driver's seat, she held it up like she'd found the Holy Grail. "Come on. We've got to get going." Honey reached over and picked up a cell phone off the passenger floorboard. "Another Christmas miracle."

"We can call Chase and Enigma. Maybe the Grass Valley Police." She reached in and tried to relieve her of the phone, only to have it jerked away. "I need to see how they are."

"You need to get in the car."

"Give me the phone."

Honey turned the key in the ignition and put it in reverse then backed it out after pulling the door shut. Tessa ran after her and banged her fist on the hood, when the car abruptly stopped. Her feet hit a patch of ice, and she found herself sprawled near the front tire. The sound of the engine revving up caused her to scramble to her feet, only to fall again next to the driver's door. The glass squeaked down, dropping a pile of snow on Tessa's upturned face.

"Yes?" Honey said coolly. "Can I help you?"

Slapping at the snow over her eyes and nose, Tessa tried once more to rise. She glared at her new partner in crime then made her way around the car to climb inside.

"That's a good girl."

"Shut up."

~ ~ ~ ~

Chase inspected their handiwork. He had to admit, the boys possessed a devious side he admired. Would it be too soon to put them on the radar of the folks at Langley or the Pentagon? Even their little sister, Heather, came up with a few good ideas to stop the warmongers that would soon storm the castle. He caught a glimpse of them in the mirror, standing behind him with their arms crossed over their chests, feet spread apart and their lower lips stuck out, resembling MacArthur wading ashore in the Philippines. All they needed were the sunglasses. He realized he also resembled the famous general, and the children were imitating him, not MacArthur.

"You guys got any sunglasses?" He walked over and pulled his out of the inside pocket of the leather jacket he'd worn earlier and slowly placed them on his nose.

They nodded and scampered upstairs to their rooms. It sounded a great deal like thunder as they rejoined him at the bottom of the steps. Each one put on their glasses as if ready for inspection. Sean Patrick's were mirrored aviators, much like his. Daniel's were black rimmed with a subtle insignia that indicated they were either connected to Harry Potter or the rebellion in Star Wars.

And then there were Heather's. She struggled to get them on straight, so Chase reached down and gave them a twist to adjust the lopsided shape.

"What are these, Heather?"

"My sunglasses."

The boys snickered.

"They look like bunny ears."

"That's because they are. I have a hat to match. Wanna see?"

"No. Do you have any real sunglasses that are a little more intimidating?"

"Intimidating? I have some reindeer ones my Mimi sent." She smiled up at him with expectation.

"I think I'll get you guys real glasses for Christmas. The kind special forces wear."

"Cool," the boys chorused. Heather hesitated but joined in their excitement.

He refocused on their creations. With any luck, whoever planned on coming after him would be slowed down long enough for him to disarm them. Would there be one or two? Thugs or professionals? Armed or brute force? And who would be behind such an attack? Although it was true, he'd made enemies over the years, a lot of them were no longer sucking oxygen. The others were in a secret black site enjoying the repetitive questions of interrogators with numbers instead of names. The possibility meant armed thugs hired to do someone else's dirty work.

"Chase, our outside lights just went dark," Sean said using his index finger to peek behind a sheer curtain. The inside lights flickered three times before also going dark.

CHAPTER TWELVE

❧◦❧◦◦❧◦◦❧◦◦❧◦◦❧

Get away from the window," Chase ordered. Sean Patrick complied and joined his siblings. He moved more cautiously to the window and took a look. What if they opened fire and the kids got in the way? He reached for his cell phone as he rejoined them in the hallway. "Where's my phone?" He stretched his neck to peer into the kitchen.

The boys shrugged. Heather stuck out her lip and batted her eyes.

"Heather, do you have my phone? I laid it down on the countertop in the kitchen." He stroked her hair and forced himself to sound calm. "You're not in trouble."

She nodded and pointed to the powder room. "It jumped out of my hand into the potty."

Chase hurried toward the room with the kids, all following while screeching, "Yuk. Gross. Ewww."

The black rectangle floated like a dead goldfish.

"I flushed first, Chasey. Promise."

He reached in for the rescue. Water dripped from the phone. Even though Enigma had these made to continue to operate under severe conditions, he wasn't sure something like death by potty meant a sure thing of resurrection. Grabbing a towel, he dried the phone off before trying to connect to the outside world.

Nothing.

Maybe it needed to reboot after it got over the shock of a little girl's clumsiness and curiosity. He checked the landline, but it, too, was dead. Someone was already closing in to do him harm. The lights flickered, and the three children jammed up against him, circling his legs with their arms.

"Okay, knights."

Heather cleared her throat with irritation.

"And, Your Majesty, it's time to take action. I'm going to get Sean's baseball bat and take a look around outside. As soon as I shut the door, you lock it and barricade yourself in your mom's room. I'll climb up the trellis and come in the window when I'm done."

The boys nodded like good little soldiers.

"Push the dresser in front of the door. I already took out the drawers so it would be lighter, but it still may take all of you. Then put the drawers back in and move whatever you can in front of the dresser. Understand?" More nods. "If everything is all clear, I'll sneak into your neighbors', the Ervins, house and call the police."

The Ervins also worked for Enigma, but Tessa's husband remained clueless to that fact. They'd become loving grandparents to these kids and watched after them when their mother did work for the president. The extra layer of protection helped Tessa to take the president up on his job offer. They never passed up a chance to watch the children, being without any of their own. The couple had planned the outing for weeks to celebrate their anniversary and nearly canceled when Tessa needed to pick her parents up at the airport. Chase had volunteered to run interference. He remembered thinking; how hard could it be? Now, he knew.

"They don't have a landline anymore, Chase," Daniel announced. "They got tired of those robo-calls trying to forgive their college loan debt or was it credit card debt?" He took a deep breath and shrugged. "I'm betting they took their cell phones."

The sound of Tessa's large wind chimes banged against the side of the house, followed by a thud. Chase had slipped out earlier and positioned it to a trip wire to alert him of any trouble.

"It's showtime." He slipped back into his coat and pulled a dark sock hat he'd found in the closet, over his head. "Are we good?"

He got three thumbs-up. Sean Patrick pulled out a walkie-talkie from under his shirt and handed it to Chase. "I set the channels in case you need us." The voice sounded so matter-of-fact, he had to remind himself Sean Patrick was still a kid. "Remember, you're Silent Knight, I'm Die Hard."

"Die Hard? You shouldn't be watching those movies."

"Mom said we could watch Christmas movies. She didn't say which ones," he smirked.

"I'm thinking she meant A Charlie Brown Christmas or Miracle on 34th Street."

"Whatever. Anyway, Daniel is Yoda since he seems to know everything."

"What about me?" Heather clapped her hands in delight.

Chase tapped her on the nose. "You are Princess Moonlight of the Everlasting Forest." He zipped up his coat and headed to the front door.

The electricity remained off for now. The lights on the Christmas tree no longer sparkled, but the lights on the mantel garland, and fake candles in the window, run by batteries gave enough light to make the kids feel a little more comfortable about being separated from him. The decorative lights on the outdoor shrubs and trees had been extinguished. He picked up the bat and headed to the door with the kids at his heels.

"When I go out…"

"We bolt the door and run to Mommy's room," Heather chirped.

Chase felt pride surge through him. All this warm, fuzzy emotion messed with his no-nonsense, take-charge way of doing things. The people he usually worked with all had a job and executed it to perfection. Even Tessa finally showed improvement. But these kids were a liability. So many things could go wrong. If anything happened to them…

The bolt locked behind him. He waited to leave the wraparound porch after listening for anything out of the ordinary. Since he knew where the noise he'd heard inside the house originated, he moved in that direction, his baseball bat ready. But there was nothing but a few footprints indicating whoever had been lurking wore boots. The wind chime now lay in a tangled mess on the juniper.

A second pair of boot prints appeared not more than three steps away, leading toward the backyard. Careful to keep an eye on the area behind him in case another person circled around, Chase continued until he reached the white picket fence. The gate had been pushed open, wide enough for a man to slip through, causing the snow to mound up, preventing it from being completely open.

Now he knew several things. Whoever these men were, they might be too lazy or out of shape to jump over the low fence. They didn't know him, or they would have expected him to be alert to changes in his environment. Whoever hired them must have neglected to tell them he'd been an Army Ranger then later a Delta Force officer. Could this be a warning of things to come? Did the enemy expect him to take out these problems and let his guard down? Knowing you were being hunted meant you second-guessed everything until you made mistakes. He'd been taking care of problems long enough to know how to avoid such traps. Whoever decided to snoop around would learn a hard lesson tonight.

He squeezed through the open gate and followed the footprints. When he neared the corner of the house, a man stepped out, looking toward the yard. Chase stepped up and tapped him on the shoulder. The man spun around and yelped at the same time. The intruder's eyes went cold, and he'd started to lift an arm when he received an uppercut to the chin with a baseball bat, causing the man to spew several teeth into the air. Before the man could catch his breath, Chase delivered a kick to the man's crotch, sending him into spasms of pain while he groped himself. Before he could make enough much noise to alert anyone else, Chase squatted down and shoved the man's sock hat in his mouth.

"Take that out of your mouth, and my next swing is at your head." Chase let him moan and nod he understood. Tears trailed from the corners of his eyes as he continued to rub his crotch and roll from side to side. "How many more are here?" When he didn't answer right away, Chase reared back with the bat, and the man held up three fingers.

This information told him whoever sent these guys knew one or two people wouldn't be able to take him down. The man before him appeared to be in his early thirties in spite of the Mohawk haircut. Chase grabbed him by the front of his lightweight jacket, quite a choice of wardrobe in the current weather and another clue the man was an idiot then jerked him to his feet. He shook his head, trying to loosen the sock hat in his mouth as Chase pushed him, face-first into a tree limb, heavy with snow. It immediately dropped onto the stranger. Pulling out the zip ties left over from earlier in the evening, he quickly secured his hands before attaching them to another limb with a bicycle chain he'd found in the garage.

The man-made guttural protests, probably in hopes of alerting his partners. Unfortunately for him, his captor lost patience and gave him a slam of the bat to the kidneys, making him lose footing and causing even more snow to fall onto his uncovered head.

"Now, be a good boy and I'll come back for you in a bit. No more noise or I'll open your pants and drop snow down there on your manhood. I figure you got about thirty minutes before hypothermia sets in, not including frostbite. Are we good?"

The man gave a weak nod of submission as Chase moved to the end of the house, bat in hand.

Pausing at the corner, he stole a quick glance into the yard, now blanketed with a deep layer of snow. No indication of another presence, only footsteps leading back to a former storage building Tessa had turned into a place she called She-Shed-Shangri-La. He had never understood why she spent money on the project until tonight. Grabbing a few minutes to herself probably kept her from going postal.

He crouched down and stayed to the side of the yard where play structures and pine trees gave him cover enough to approach. When traces of other footsteps disappeared, he noticed they'd circled back toward the house and around to the opposite side from where he'd left the first guy. Banging on the upstairs windows of Tessa's bedroom brought him to a halt.

The children were all banging on the glass, yelling and pointing. He felt a sudden rush of anger at their noisemaking until Sean Patrick managed to raise the window and shout, "Behind you!"

In the middle of a quick pivot, the smack of a shovel hit him upside the head and he fell to the ground. A fog settled in his brain.

A gruff voice said, "Leave him. He ain't goin' anywhere. We need to shut those kids up before they wake the dead. We'll finish this in a few minutes."

Darkness moved over his eyes, and he fought to avoid unconsciousness. He got to his hands and knees and shook off the pain on his ear. They had only stunned him by hitting him in a sensitive area. It took effort, but he managed to get to his feet. The bat lay deep in the snow, and he was grateful they hadn't taken it. He staggered at first, trying to follow their steps then stopped before rounding the house to see if the children were still watching, but they weren't. He could scamper up the lattice, but stopping the intruders before they entered the house would be a better option.

The snowdrifts were deeper here because of the wind and slowed him down. The footsteps stopped under the dining room windows—where the glass had been broken out and had made little patterns in the snow below. His heart jumped into his throat.

The intruders were in the house with the children.

CHAPTER THIRTEEN

There's no answer," Tessa groaned. "Why isn't Chase picking up?" She squeezed the phone and shook it. "What was I thinking, leaving him in charge of my kids?"

Honey started the car. "Ahh, purrs like a kitten." After backing out of the spot, she eased into the lane between the parking lots. "I do love your American motor cars." She pulled into an empty area and contacted the GPS service for best directions to Grass Valley. The news wasn't good. While she drummed her fingers on the steering wheel, Honey stared out the windshield, her eyes glazing over.

"We can't continue to sit here. Someone might recognize the car and then we're toast. Probably has a tracking device on it." She tried dialing Chase again but got the same result. "They're in trouble. I know it." She rubbed her face in frustration. "Who would be after him, and how did you find out the information?"

"Connections," she mumbled as her finger-drumming continued. "Need-to-know basis."

"You're no different than all the others at Enigma, all cloak and dagger."

"Call your buddies at Enigma, and maybe they can send support. Their weather in Sacramento has to be better than here. We'll go as far as we can."

"They aren't going to let us onto the highway without tire chains and four-wheel drive." She dialed Enigma headquarters and got a no-service signal along with a message of a low battery. "Nothing. This thing is worthless. Someone has my phone and can possibly call the moon and have enough battery life to go into the next millennium."

The finger-drumming stopped. "I sense frustration."

"Ya think?" Tessa banged the back of her head against the headrest. Her eyes caught movement ahead of them at the same time Honey put the car in reverse and looked through the rear window.

"We got company. Hold on." Honey whipped the car around as if she'd done this kind of thing before.

"Oh. My. Gosh," Tessa yelled as a dark Hummer barreled toward them. "Go faster. Faster."

"Glove box. Get it out."

Tessa wasn't sure what "it" was, but she followed orders. When their car swerved hard right to make it go forward, her head bounced off the window. "Ouch!" Once more she fumbled with the glove box and found a Smith & Wesson 1076 with several cartridges. She'd practiced on one early in her training. She grabbed it as the rear window shattered with gunshots. A fleeting thought of how Honey knew a weapon would be in there would be addressed later.

"They're coming up fast. Do you know how to use that?" Honey demanded.

Tessa felt as if she'd slipped into a dream state, where this was the result of not enough sleep and too much stress.

"Tessa, snap out of it. You've got to stop them. Shoot, damn it!"

When the back glass exploded inward, something snapped inside her. The woman's commands brought her out of her trance long enough to turn in her seat. She took off the safety, and pulled the trigger once, nearly dropping it because of the recoil.

"Hey! Both hands, cupcake," Honey fumed.

She unbuckled her seat belt to be able to twist around and get a clear shot. "Could you drive a little more safely? I undid my seat belt."

The Irish assassin flashed her an incredulous glare.

"Oh. Never mind. We can talk about this later." She sounded too mom-like in the moment.

"Shoot!"

Tessa clenched her teeth, narrowed her eyes, and fired. The approaching vehicle's windshield shattered. The attack car backed off then swerved and hit another parked car and over-corrected. It careened sideways, jumped a median, and crashed into a tree.

"Way to go, my sweet little Grass Valley commando." Honey continued to drive, but reached out to pat Tessa's hip as she flipped herself around and reloaded the weapon before buckling up. "Uh-oh." A loud pop, and the car was wobbling. "Guess they hit one of our tires, no, two. We're on foot now." She pulled off the road, put the car into park, and hopped out. "I see flashing lights so be quick about it."

"Maybe the police can help us." Tessa climbed out as Honey disappeared into the small park alongside the road. She reached back inside the car and took out another cartridge from the glove box. Stuffing it in her purse, she scrambled after her partner in crime.

Honey let her catch up. "And how would you explain stealing an FBI car?"

"I'd tell them the truth, of course."

Honey smirked and picked up her pace. "We deal in deception, not truth. Do you really want to spend Christmas in jail?"

"I want to go home," she yelled.

The assassin halted so fast, Tessa ran into her. "Then do as I say. We've got to prevent whoever is after Chase from reaching him. These guys are after me because they know I can help him. Not sure how they picked up my trail. I'm very careful." She turned to press onward.

"Why are they after him?"

"Dunno."

"You must know more than you're telling me," she growled. "You don't strike me as anyone who is ever in the dark about anything."

"Okay. Maybe. He made an enemy years ago but couldn't do anything about it. The guy is very high profile and protected, even well respected. Chase let it go because of the demands of war and the special ops he did. He was an angry mess when I met him.

Director Clark gave him focus with Enigma work. Two months ago, Chase started poking around again to see where things were with this guy."

"Who is it?"

"More important is why now? Why would this creep even care? Chase must have struck a nerve. He's a private citizen, not an enemy combatant or part of a terrorist cell, although Chase might have a different opinion of that fact. I believe he uncovered information that will give him a way into his organization and finish him off. Private citizens are safe from Enigma unless they pose a threat to American interests and security."

"In other words, you might not like the big prescription companies, jacked-up oil prices over holiday weekends or social media giants, the current political incumbents, but sometimes life sucks and we have no other choice but to take it."

"Exactly. Whoever we're dealing with fell in one of those benign categories. Besides if the world thinks you walk on water, there is a certain do-no-harm bubble people put you in. Beloved and above the law in some cases."

"Who. Is. It?"

"Honestly, I dunno. Chase always played close to the vest with anything concerning this guy. He called him Satan's spawn most of the time. That's all I know." Honey reached out and grabbed Tessa's arm then jerked her down on the ground behind tall evergreen bushes. "Police." They zipped by and then backed up when they saw the Escalade. The Hummer appeared to be causing even more attention. "Guess you'd be opposed to taking a police car?"

The assassin started to stand up, but Tessa tugged her back down. "Absolutely not. We're in over our head now."

"Where's your spirit of adventure?" Honey grunted as she continued to survey the area around them. "Come on. I think I have an idea."

Both women kept to the darkest areas in the park. The snow softened the sounds of their progress until they crossed the street to a gas station resembling a building from the Old West. It was decked out with lots of bright lights and a giant cowboy boot with a purple lizard on it that moved its head from side to side.

"You Americans do tacky better than anyone."

Tessa had to agree but said nothing that might slow their progress. Inside the station, an area the size of a large grocery store, the smell of evergreen and stale tacos made her a little nauseous. A clerk mopped the melted snow around a sign warning of slippery surfaces. The song, "Let It Snow" could be heard over the slot machines in an adjacent bar and grill decorated to imitate an Old West saloon. Clouds of cigarette smoke wafted out into the store where two men wearing down jackets and state highway caps glanced at them and wolf-whistled when they had to step around them.

"You ladies are out awful late. Working?"

Tessa started to give an angry retort at the implication when Honey pivoted and leveled a very disarming smile. She eyed them head to toe then fluffed her strawberry-blonde hair with the very red tips. Talk about tacky.

"Well, you boys look like you've been working hard"—her gaze fell on their crotches— "this snowy evening."

"We sure have," a burly one cooed. "Getting ready to clear the interstate. Snow stopped up there on the mountain."

"I bet you big strong fellas needed a little break." Honey elbowed Tessa, and she took a step back.

"Let's go," she said, grabbing the assassin's arm. "We don't have time for this."

"Now hold on there, Miss High and Mighty," the younger one said as he patted Tessa's cheek. She slapped away his hand that smelled of onions. "Oh, I like feisty."

"Do you like a foot up your—"

Honey laughed playfully and hugged Tessa. "She plays hard to get. Our last—customer decided he couldn't handle her and stormed off without paying a dime."

"What?" Tessa fumed.

"Tomorrow our rent is due, and she needs half." Honey ran her hand down the front of the burly man's jacket. "Wouldn't want to make a donation, would you?"

They both grinned and rubbed the stubble on their chins.

"Well maybe." The one with onion hands pointed to Tessa. "The shy ones are always the wild ones. I left my wallet out in my snowplow, if you know what I mean." He winked.

Tessa suddenly realized they were about to steal yet another vehicle but at what cost? She took a deep breath and forced a smile on the younger man. "You're kinda cute." She felt like she was speaking with a mouth full of cardboard. The urge to puke almost got the best of her.

Honey slid her arm through the burly man's and squeezed it close to her body. "I bet your nickname is snowplow—if you know what I mean." They both laughed good-naturedly as the four of them moved toward the automatic doors.

They walked out to the parking lot near the back of the gas station and waited for each man to unlock his snowplow.

"Can you start them up so we'll be warm? We've been walking around in the weather for hours. I'm sure I would be even more appreciative with a warm tush, Mr. Snowplow." Again, Honey offered a coy smile.

"You got it, girls."

Both men hurried to start their engines.

"Play nice, Tessa. We can take the truck over the pass and plow a path all the way to Grass Valley. By the time we get to Nevada City, the California Highway Department will have done our work for us. Easy. It's almost midnight." She tapped Tessa on her lips with a gloved finger. "Lick those chapped lips. Be seductive." Tessa pulled away when she reached for her purse.

"These places have landlines. Let's just go call for help."

"Then we'd be on security for sure, and who knows who would be listening."

"Paranoid."

"In my line of work, it pays to be paranoid. Besides, I don't want some greasy clerk giving us the once-over so he'll have a good description on the off chance their cameras are down. Which is a real possibility. Trust me. I know what I'm doing."

"You have all the answers, don't you?" Tessa snarled as Honey again tried to take the purse.

"Give me the damn gun before you hurt yourself. I may need it first. This truck is in better shape than the other one. See the tires? And the guy is twice my size."

"And what am I supposed to do. Wait for you to come rescue me from being sexually assaulted by the other creep?"

"I'm sure you'll think of something. You've lasted this long at Enigma without getting your head shot off. Surely you've learned a few tricks." Honey grinned and elbowed her good-naturedly. "Tricks. Get it?"

"What I've learned is if there is trouble, you show up to the party."

Honey snatched Tessa's purse, quickly removed the gun, and slipped it in her deep coat pocket.

"I'm not doing this." Tessa shivered. "I feel like I need a bath."

"A bath?" the burly man asked as he climbed down out of his truck. "Little motel down the road has heart-shaped Jacuzzis in every room. Maybe when we get done here, we'll go freshen up," he said, nudging his friend as he walked up. He rubbed his hands up and down the sides of his coveralls.

The younger man nodded toward his truck then reached for Tessa. "Come on, sweetheart." He switched to a Clint Eastwood impersonation. "I'm here to make your day."

"I seriously doubt that, you sexually frustrated Neanderthal."

Before Tessa knew what was happening, the man slapped her to the ground. She tasted blood and tried to get to her feet, but he reached down and jerked her to upright. He shook her violently and dragged her away while she kicked and clawed at any areas she could reach. Through his thick clothing, he probably couldn't feel a thing.

The other man laughed and called after them. "When I'm done with the redhead, I'll come help you. Save me some."

She twisted away and was headed back when Honey pulled out the gun and shot her mark in the head, propelling him backward.

"Asshole. You shouldn't have messed with my friend." She kicked snow on the man then leveled the gun at the other one as Tessa fell at her feet. "Get up," Honey ordered.

The second man halted, threw his hands up, and backed away. "Don't shoot."

"Fine. But you're driving us over the mountains."

"I can't," he whined.

Honey raised the gun a little higher and fired, slicing off part of his ear. "Next time I'll take your pecker off and shove it down your throat."

"Okay. Okay. I'll drive you. Please don't kill me. I got a family."

"A family," Tessa yelled. "We don't need them. Shoot him. We can drive ourselves."

Honey fired twice, and Tessa screamed.

The man fell facedown in the snow, and a circle of blood formed.

"What have you done?" Tessa ran over to take a look.

"You said shoot him." Honey returned the weapon to her pocket then checked both men for any identification. Next, she removed anything that made them look like drivers for the state. She tossed Tessa a cap.

"I only wanted to scare him."

"Oh good. I think I did my job quite well, don't you? Come on. We need to hide these bodies."

CHAPTER FOURTEEN

Chase prayed the kids were secure and hadn't left their mother's room. He climbed through the open window then dropped to the floor. From the sounds of fumbling in the dark and a lack of leadership, he could take these clowns out before any real damage was done.

Pulling out the walkie-talkie, he tried to contact Sean Patrick. "Die Hard. This is Silent Knight. Do you copy?"

"Silent Knight, this is Die Hard. We copy."

He slipped through the dining room and spotted two of the men climbing the steps. His heart stopped when he spotted the glow of a flashlight at the top.

"Die Hard! Get your people back inside the bedroom. That's an order," he growled no louder than a whisper.

"Sorry, Silent Knight. You're breaking up," he lied.

He rushed out to intervene, but something pinged and bounced rapidly down the stairs toward the intruders. Chase bumped the hall table, knocking over a collection of wooden Santas and a bowl of glass Christmas balls. The crashing and popping reminded him of incoming mortar attacks in Afghanistan for a few seconds.

With the sudden explosion of glass, wood, and what he now knew to be marbles cascading down the steps, the intruders pivoted awkwardly to look back at him. Their next step made contact with several marbles, and they flapped their arms like flamingos taking flight. Their weapons flew up in the air as did their feet, and they were soon rolling down the steps with grunts and confused expressions.

Chase lunged forward with the bat and swung toward any body part he could reach. The first intruder dodged a blow to the head but caught the strike against his shoulder, laying him out flat. The second man scampered up and tried to move away but stepped on a handful of marbles and fell flat on his face. He remained out of reach, and Chase needed to avoid the marbles if possible.

The third man now had circled back and dragged his downed partner away by tugging on the back of his collar. They disappeared into the kitchen where only a battery-operated candle lit the room.

The children squatted, peering expectedly through the bars of the railing. He motioned for them to return to their mother's bedroom, but they merely gave him a thumbs-up. It was too dark to see their expressions in spite of the glow of the flashlight now resting on the floor beside Sean Patrick. Finally, he growled in a whisper for them to turn off the flashlight. In seconds, the light extinguished.

The man on the floor moaned and tried to sit up, and outlines of the other two men appeared in the kitchen. Thankfully, they hadn't found the door that would have allowed them to circle back through the living room, catching him off guard in the hall. He guessed the reason they didn't rush forward had to do with not knowing where the scattered marbles on the floor might be located.

His immediate concern was whether these two had guns. When they'd gone airborne seconds earlier, he couldn't see where their weapons had landed or if they had been able to scoop them up. The one'd he tied up had nothing, not even a pocket knife. That indicated he might be nothing but a thug trying to rob folks at Christmas. These guys had amateur written all over them. A fleeting thought darted in and out of his mind that these were not the ones come to take him out. With the break-ins in other parts of the neighborhood, these guys could be a part of a home invasion ring. Christmas was a time when people went to parties, children participated in programs at school and church, and you visited family away from home, all while leaving a treasure trove of gifts, electronics, and jewelry behind.

"Better put the bat down before we have to shoot you," one of the men said, stepping forward.

"I'll take my chances," Chase said as he evaluated their movements. "I'd really like it if you tried to take it from me."

The two paused. They tilted their heads toward their unmoving friend on the floor, but one reached in his pocket for something. Chase reached down and jerked their friend to his feet to pose like a shield. At the same time, a taser in the man's hand came out and let loose two projectiles that attached to their friend's chest. Chase dropped him immediately so not to be affected by the jolt. Freed, he twisted and shook, driving his friends back farther into the kitchen.

"Chase! Catch!" Daniel tossed a slingshot to him. "The table!"

Chase caught the weapon with his free hand and looked to his right at the small table that belonged to Tessa's grandmother. A jar of mismatched buttons with the lid lying on the side offered more ammo. He forced the bat under one arm then grabbed a handful of buttons.

"Get back in the bedroom," Chase yelled at the kids as he charged forward.

This time the intruders stopped, and Chase found himself flanked by two of them. They wore sinister snarls. They lunged at Chase with doubled fists and connected to his side and kidney. Buttons scattered on the floor when he staggered back.

He managed to swing the bat, although it connected only with a few of Tessa's foo-foo decorations on the counter, but the crash startled them enough that they stepped away. Even though pain surged up through his back, he pulled the bat back for another swing.

"This guy is crazy. Let's get out of here," number two said.

He cut them off and held the bat like it might be a loaded cannon waiting to go off. "Who sent you? Who are you working for?"

They glanced at each other and ran for the back door, but Chase slammed one of them on the back of the knees, and he crashed over the granite countertop. After pushing off, he whirled around with a banshee yell and came at Chase with doubled fists. Number one ran around the table and toward the hall as Chase swung the bat, only to have it caught in midair by him and jerked from his hands. For a split second the intruder appeared surprised that he managed to take it as he examined the weapon in his hands

In a split-second decision, Chase pulled out the slingshot from his pocket and several jacks from the forbidden package Heather had given him earlier. She had opened it and poured them into one of the Christmas bowls on the counter. He snapped the shot and connected with the man's eye. With the intruder temporarily blinded, Chase landed a punch to the man's gut followed by an uppercut to the chin, and the villain dropped the bat. He caught it before it hit the floor and grabbed the man by the nose and threw him forward toward his friend. He staggered then picked up speed.

The intruders were barreling toward the front door when a slight movement on each side of the hall caught his eye. The boys were waiting, one in the living room, the other on the edge of the dining room. Sean's voice boomed like that of a former drill sergeant he'd once had when he went into the Rangers.

They pulled a rope tight across the floor, as little Heather's hands swung the front door open. The intruders slipped on something before snagging their feet in the rope and fell forward through the door. When they hit the patches of frozen snow, they slid toward the steps.

Chase jumped over their rope and ran to the door where he managed to swing Heather to the side then proceeded outside. The men groaned as they struggled to get to their knees. Two familiar faces appeared at both of the steps, leveling their weapons. It was the cops from earlier in the evening.

"Officers," Chase said calmly.

"You again. I'm beginning to think you attract trouble," one officer said as the other reached down and cuffed the intruders.

The children ran out and hugged Chase's legs so tightly he thought he might fall over. "It's okay, guys. You all right?" Their heads nodded, and their arms squeezed tighter around his legs and waist. "Officer, there's another one inside on the floor. They had a taser. Missed me and hit him."

One officer arched an eyebrow. "Lucky for you."

"There's another one tied to a tree on the side of the house. He's probably getting a little cold." He reached down and lifted Heather up in his arms. She immediately put a choke-hold hug around his neck and wrapped her legs around his waist. "How come you're here again?"

The second officer led the tased intruder out of the house in handcuffs and grinned at Chase. "Your neighbor lady, a few doors down, Bridgette, I think. She was watching out her window and noticed these guys slipping around the house. She knew you were here with the kids. Said you two had a connection?"

Chase rolled his eyes then dropped his free hand on Daniel's head. "Be sure to thank her for me. I've kind of got my hands full here. But thanks again for your help. Guess I'll be coming in to explain this in the morning, too."

"I'd appreciate it if we didn't have to post a guard here for the rest of the night."

He fished a card out of his jeans pocket and handed it over. "What's this?" The officer looked down at it for a few seconds before raising his eyes to Chase. He seemed to stand a little more at attention.

"Call that number for me, and they'll help you out. If you ever need anything, let me know. I owe you."

The officer elbowed his partner and showed him the card. His eyes got a little rounder as they lifted to meet Chase's. "Yes, sir. Glad we could be of help. Second thought, maybe we should leave someone at the entrance gate?"

"I'd rather you get that piece of trash tied to the tree out of here. These kids have had enough excitement for one night. Oh, and can you get the power company to get our electric back on?" He started toward the door, Heather still in his arms.

"Right away."

"Thanks, and Merry Christmas."

"Merry Christmas, sir."

He didn't miss the new level of respect in their voices.

"Come on, kids. I'm guessing we made a mess that needs to be cleaned up."

CHAPTER FIFTEEN

The snowplow roared to life. Honey let out a shout of enthusiasm followed by childlike laughter. After wiggling to adjust her position behind the wheel, she examined all the bells and whistles of her new toy.

"Have you ever driven a big truck like this before?" Tessa hissed.

She couldn't believe she'd helped the Irish assassin drag the two men into the bushes. It proved a difficult task, considering one was tall and the other, rotund. It took both of them to get the job done. Honey took care of hiding the blood trail.

"You know there are security cameras everywhere." Tessa palmed her forehead. "We'll probably be featured on the morning news, with the police parading us around in orange jumpsuits."

"Orange really isn't my color," confessed Honey.

"Maybe horizontal black stripes, then. The police are looking for us."

"They're looking for someone. Those security cameras in the back of the station were disabled. The motion sensors never even blinked. Besides, there were no lightbulbs."

"Well, there were cameras inside, and we were seen leaving with those jerks." Tessa checked the side mirrors for trouble.

"Maybe you can get your little tech buddy at Enigma...what's his name?"

"Vernon Kemp."

"Yeah. That's the fella. Have him go in and do his thing."

"And how do you suppose I do that without a phone?" She puffed out a burst of air. "There will be hell to pay because I lost another Enigma phone. Whoever has it will have all my contacts."

"Come on, sweetness. Surely Enigma put a kind of failsafe on such a sensitive piece of equipment."

Tessa knew that to be the case. Only her breath could activate any call, and her touch enabled the second layer of protection. She'd once thought having such a device would make her life easier. Now she feared someone might have a chance to hack into the database—if that was even possible. With any luck, whoever took the phone tried to get in, and alerts went out like someone storming Area 51. Vernon would backtrack her movements and hopefully figure out she needed help.

"I guess you're right. Our biggest concern right now is getting in touch with Chase and letting him know we're on our way. I want to know my kids are safe."

"One more little concern."

"What now?"

"We have company. The police are coming up behind us."

Tessa caught sight of them in the side mirror then glanced over at Honey whose lips curved up in a smile. "Holy Moly. Why are you smiling? What are you about to do?"

"Have a little fun is all. You buckled?"

"No. No. No. No," Tessa said scrambling to find her seat belt. "Dear Jesus, save me!"

~ ~ ~ ~

With the children sitting at the breakfast bar eating scrambled eggs and cinnamon toast, Chase returned to the porch to watch the second police car arrive to help with the prisoners. The officer he'd given the business card strolled over to speak to him.

"Thought you'd like to know this appears to be an organized theft ring law enforcement has been tracking in Sacramento. They've been inching toward Nevada county for a couple of months. Each of these guys have a record. They've hit three neighborhoods in the last week. Lucky you were here to stop them." He grinned. "That first bunch we took in were most likely working with them. We'll know more in the morning."

"And you know this because?"

"The frozen one you tied outside asked if we had them, too." He chuckled. "Nothing like a dumb criminal."

Chase extended his hand. "Thanks again for showing up. Appreciate your service."

"Seems to me I should be thanking you for all your service. You have a Merry Christmas." The officer started down the steps then came back and handed him a piece of paper. "Almost forgot. Told to give you this from someone named Vernon Kemp. Came in over the radio a little while ago."

Chase nodded and slipped the paper in his pocket as the yard lights came on. The Christmas lights now twinkled inside the house as well.

The children finished the food he'd prepared for them and carried their plates to the sink. He was surprised to observe they rinsed them off and stuck them in the dishwasher, with Sean Patrick rearranging a few things to make everything fit. Daniel added the dishwasher detergent and turned it to start. Although Heather missed a few spots with her limited reach, she wiped down the counter where they'd sat. The idea they were used to chores impressed him with Tessa's parenting.

He doubted it had anything to do with her husband, Robert, since he wasn't around for the important moments. What could Robert be thinking, leaving a knockout wife and three great kids alone so much? How many times had he considered making his intentions known? Once or twice he'd even toyed with the idea of making Robert disappear altogether. Unfortunately, his conscience and sense of honor prevented him from stepping over the line he'd drawn in the sand when it came to Tessa. She worked for him. Complications with a female agent only meant the mission at hand would be compromised.

"What ya thinkin', Chasey?" Heather's little voice always had the power to make him grin.

"What good soldiers you guys are."

"Are we going to play princess school now?"

The boys moaned but hushed when he held up a hand. "We

need to clean up our mess first. What did you boys throw down on the floor to make it so slick when those guys slid out like a seal on its belly?"

He looked back over his shoulder and could see residue left on the floor in the hall. The burglars had likely absorbed most of it on their slide out, but he stepped around it to avoid suffering the same fate. When he walked back to where the hardwood was a sticky mess, the children hurried after him.

"Baby oil. Mom keeps it in the powder room," Sean Patrick offered with a boyish grin. "Grabbed it when you were in the kitchen getting your butt handed to you."

Chase grabbed him in a headlock and gave him a noogie, causing the children to laugh.

"You disobeyed a direct order."

Sean Patrick pulled away and shrugged. "Good thing, too. You're kind of new at this stuff, aren't you?"

"I guess I've learned a lot from you three tonight. Maybe I should let you clean up all this mess ASAP. Now move it," he snapped.

The boys rushed toward the kitchen, but Heather stood her ground and smiled up at him.

"I don't think you were talking to me," she cooed.

It hurt to force an angry frown down on her, especially when her eyes grew wide. "You are just like your mother. Yes. I was talking to you. You disobeyed me and will help your brothers."

Her bottom lip jutted out.

"Now!"

He half expected tears but instead got a cold stare. Again. Exactly like her mother. After a pivot on tiny feet, she moved at a snail's pace down the hall toward the kitchen, stroking the head of her fluffy unicorn.

"Women," he mumbled.

While the children cleaned the floor, he wondered if the burglars had been a distraction to throw him off the real threat. Whoever planned on an attack was still out there—waiting. He needed to wrap this up and fast. He pulled the paper from his pocket and read it.

In minutes, he'd located a secondary phone Tessa had hidden in the bottom of a tampon box in her bathroom. Part of him thought it was genius especially since fishing around in a tampon box creeped him out a little. He knew she kept a loaded Beretta on top of the cabinets in the kitchen but hadn't been able to get it. The one he'd replaced in the dining room didn't have ammo, so it was useless. He needed to reprimand her for that slipup. According to the note, he needed to call in as soon as possible.

"Vernon?"

"Your tech genius is here to serve." He beamed. Chase could imagine him sitting in front of four or five computer screens, divided between gaming and national security. "Looks like you've been making friends with the Grass Valley PD."

"Yeah. Not sure they're happy about it. Glad they reached out."

"Can't send reinforcements tonight, Chase. Black ice everywhere. Sac International Airport was closed a couple of hours ago. Too slick to try and make it up to you."

"Any idea who is after me?"

"No chatter. You're not known for leaving any loose ends, Chase."

"True. Honey is sure someone is coming for me. Those guys tonight were bumbling idiots. I think they were a distraction. Maybe make me feel overconfident I'd cleaned up another mess."

"Too easy."

"Can you tie into Tessa's security here at the house and alert the police if you see anything? I've got these kids to watch, and they make my head spin. I might miss something."

"On it."

"Any word from the girls in Reno?"

"Nothing."

"I'm not sure if I should feel good about that."

"They tried calling earlier, but it was garbled. I keep trying to call them back. Hopefully, they'll reconnect to let us know what to look for. Oh. A strange call came into the answering service. Left a message for you. Strange it wasn't garbled at all. Clear as a bell, actually."

"What was the message?"

"Said Hebrew 13:2. That's it. What's it mean?"

Chase walked down the stairs and could see the kids cleaning the hallway floor with great delight and mischief.

"'Do not neglect to show hospitality to strangers, for thereby some have entertained angels unawares.'"

"Meaning?"

"Meaning Angelo is not far away."

CHAPTER SIXTEEN

Are you going to stop?" Tessa knew her voice had gotten louder as the flashing lights got closer. A devious laugh spilled from behind Honey's gritted teeth.

Their truck had reached the highway that led over the mountains. The snow fell heavier here, and the prospect of plowing the drifts created a sense of panic. What did they know about driving or plowing through a snowstorm? This could be an accident waiting to happen if Honey got it in her head to try and outrun the police.

The Reno police stopped their cars, giving the two women a chance to put needed distance between them.

"Maybe they weren't after us," Tessa said, checking the side mirror.

"They've contacted the Highway Patrol. These guys can't go over the mountain in those cars. Expect reinforcements. In the meantime, let's see what this baby will do. Come on, Tessa, have a little fun."

"Fun? There are two dead guys—"

"Well the second one might still be alive. It was your idea, so you're to blame."

Tessa let out a frustrated scream while pounding her fists against the dashboard. "News alert! You're a psycho."

Honey shrugged. "Now that hurts, coming from my best friend."

"Let's be clear about something. We are not friends. You are trouble. And if we get caught, I will be blabbing the God's truth as fast as they can write it down."

Honey turned a dead stare at her, revealing a threat of violence. "Don't threaten me, love. Being my friend is going to keep you alive...if you know what I mean."

Tessa gulped her pride along with the fear rising inside her. "Friends it is, then." Her eyelids batting away in her fear. Honey's mouth turned up in a wide smile as she reached over and pinched her cheek.

"Ahh. I'm touched. Just think we can have tea together, go shopping for weapons, shoes, of course, and maybe grab lunch while your wee ones are at school. Maybe I'll come sit in one of your classes to see what I've been missing." She snapped her fingers. "I know. Invite me to be a guest speaker. I could open the eyes of those budding socialists you teach."

Tessa wiggled back in her seat and took a few deep breaths. "It's good to have options," she mumbled. "I'll pencil you in when I get home. Next, you'll be wanting a girls' weekend."

"I think that's what we're havin'. Bet you'll remember this one."

Tessa grinned in spite of herself. "I think you may be right." Was the FBI agent at the airport after Honey? "By the way, when I tried to find you at the airport, I saw an FBI agent outside. He wouldn't be looking for you by chance?"

"And how do you know he was FBI?"

"We've had a couple of run-ins, shall we say."

"Did he see you?"

"Pretty sure he did. He looked a little surprised, so maybe——"

"I wish you'd told me earlier."

"Would that have been before I was robbed, my car got damaged, or you killed two state employees?" She groaned and palmed her forehead. "I bet it was his Escalade we stole."

"You're kind of a whiner, Tessa. Did anyone ever tell ya that?"

"Yes. Your other best friend, Samantha Cordova."

"She is no friend of mind. I don't trust her, and you shouldn't, either. I know you work together, but she's out to get you fired if not killed. She's jealous."

Dr. Samantha Cordova was a senior agent at Enigma and had been put in charge of her training. The Bataan Death March of WWII must have inspired her methods. She remained the most beautiful and lethal woman Tessa had ever met. The woman didn't miss a day or opportunity to inflict pain and humiliation on her psyche.

The only way Tessa survived the daily harassment was to make fun of her and prove over and over she had plenty to offer the team. If Samantha was jealous, it had to do with Captain Hunter intervening on her behalf from time to time. She liked being the queen bee, and having another woman to compete with didn't go over very well.

Tessa only nodded her acceptance of Honey's declaration of what she considered truth and decided to focus on the here and now.

The truck shifted gears as they continued to climb away from Reno. The two women focused on the road. Honey ignored the radio calls from the highway department and sang Christmas carols at the top of her lungs. Tessa cringed at the possibility of spending the holidays in jail. Would Enigma let such a thing happen? Of course, they would because, technically, they didn't exist.

"Will you please shut up?" Tessa adjusted the radio to hear the chatter going on about the missing truck. Most of it concerned trying to find out why they hadn't called in to give their location.

"Probably should have loaded those jerks onto the truck, dumped them up here, and covered them up with the snowplow." She quipped. "Find them in the spring."

"You're a sadistic—"

"Careful. You know I'm a little sensitive about my control issues."

"Control issues? Is that what they call it these days? You kill people for a living."

Honey threw both hands in the air, and Tessa gasped and pointed to the road.

"Well, someone has to do it. And it pays very well, I might add. Besides, I'm semi-retired. Got your family to thank for my new lease on life. They struck a tender spot deep inside me. Made me want to be better. Why, until tonight, I'd not offed anyone since—

well, since then, I guess."

"So, you're saying I'm a bad influence."

"Looks that way. But I don't hold any hard feelings toward ya for making me backslide."

"Thanks."

Honey reached over and poked Tessa's arm with a fist. "Ahh. You're welcome. I knew we'd be good friends. I don't know why everyone talks so bad about you." She shrugged and twisted her lips to the side. "For some reason, I didn't get much pleasure out of it like in the past. Hmm. Wonder why?"

Hands over her face, Tessa shook her head in frustration. "I can't believe the day I'm having. My parents are somewhere between Denver and Sacramento, my husband is stuck in Chicago, my kids are staying with a bully who runs the world like it's boot camp and probably has a hit out on him. Then there's the weather, my poor car, a questionable man of God who stole from me, and, to top it off, my sidekick is an assassin who has turned me into a fugitive."

"And you thought this was going to be boring." Honey smiled while she adjusted her mirror. "I think we might have company." Honey laid her hand on the gun inside her coat and gave a little pat while slowing down.

"So help me, Honey, if you hurt law enforcement, I'll shoot you myself."

She smiled over at Tessa. "Would ya now? My best friend has turned into quite the bad girl. You're going to make our Captain Hunter a very happy man."

"What's the plan?" Tessa growled and slapped Honey's arm with the back of her hand, drawing another devious smile. "I see a roadblock up ahead. There's an exit before that. We could pull over and surrender."

"Good idea."

"What? Really?" She took a deep breath. "Finally. The voice of reason."

"You're such a bad influence, Tessa Scott."

The snowplow slowed and took the exit with the Highway Patrol car following. A second one appeared and moved ahead of them at a faster pace. It didn't take long for the second car to stop at an angle, blocking the road leading into what Tessa thought might be the small town of Truckee. She felt confused since she'd not ever been on this particular road.

"Okay. Pull your ski mask down farther and tuck those curls up inside. Can you pretend to be a new driver? Don't look so adorable."

Tessa nodded.

"Here we go."

"What? I thought we were going to surrender?"

"Well, what does surrender really mean these days?" She grabbed what looked like identification papers and work orders off the dashboard.

"It means to capitulate, give in, give oneself up, yield, concede, submit, give way, defer, acquiesce, back down, cave in, relent, succumb, quit, crumble. Does any of that ring a bell?"

"Oh. Guess I misunderstood. You Americans and so many fancy words."

Honey brought the snowplow to an idling position and pulled her own ski mask down, with the state highway insignia showing above her eyebrows. Both women had stripped the men of their jackets before too much blood soaked them. They didn't appear to be state issued, since they were different colors of burgundy. Inside the trucks were fluorescent vests they slipped on over the coats.

"Do you think this coat makes me look fat?" Honey asked offhandedly as she ran her hands down the front. Tessa glared at her, hoping to convey irritation at her lackadaisical attitude toward their current situation. "Relax. We'll be okay. A walk in the park, as you Americans like to say in the movies. Been in deeper—"

A rap on the door caused Tessa to jump.

Honey grinned. "Showtime. Remember. We're tough, and this is no big deal." She rolled down the window. "Good evening, Officer."

~ ~ ~ ~

The cell phone vibrated in Chase's pants pocket. He pointed to some scattered toys in the living room for Heather to pick up and then toward the marbles scattered below the steps for the boys to gather up. Then he answered, "I'm listening."

"Chase, there's a report a snowplow was commandeered at a

convenience store. The girls were spotted on security not far from there. According to the locator on Tessa's car, it hasn't moved."

"Snowplow? What are you talking about, Vernon?"

"When they left the casino, they were caught on camera several times. For whatever reason, they didn't take the car. I was able to figure out the direction they went by tapping into the security in the area."

"This is starting to sound like you're going to give me bad news."

"Yes, sir. They entered the convenience store and talked to two men in state highway gear."

"Did their faces show?"

"Not much. But it was Honey. Mostly, she kept her back to the camera. Tessa seemed to be mouthing at her. To Honey's credit, she remained calm and in control. A few minutes later, they walked out with the men."

"What about the plows?"

"One of them is missing, and the two men haven't checked in or answered their cell phones or truck radios. I'm guessing the girls stole it."

"Can you go in and delete any footage of them coming and going over the last few hours?"

"Already done. There's a roadblock on the mountain. I'm trying to patch into their communication system so I can listen in. Be easier if I knew which truck they stole. Working on the info now."

"And who might be after me?"

"No clue. The only one who seems to be not a fan and is still alive is the tribesman, but we know he's playing nice with the Russians right now and up to his neck in a double life. Besides, he thinks you're more of a nuisance than a threat."

Chase chewed the inside of his bottom lip as he considered the possibility the man, Roman Darya, Petrov, aka the tribesman, might be planning an attempt on his life. That wouldn't be his style, and Petrov knew Tessa would never forgive him if harm came to any Enigma agent. The two had a history, and Chase figured the only reason the unpredictable agent hadn't made a move against him was due to his infatuation with Tessa, whom he'd kidnapped and brainwashed a year earlier.

"No. It isn't the tribesman. He wouldn't sneak around if he

wanted me dead. Besides, he'd much rather have me suffer at the thought of him taking Tessa again."

"Know anyone in the Bilderbergers?" The secretive group continued to inspire conspiracy theories from the left and right about their agenda. In reality, it bolstered a consensus around free markets of Western capitalism and its interests around the globe.

"No. Why?" Chase knew they came from all walks of life, such as political leaders, experts in industry, science, finance, academia, and the media. He wondered at times if they weren't the real money behind Enigma.

"That Angelo guy appears to be everywhere. He managed to become a CEO of a big European tech company several years ago. Made a killing in the market and left them high and dry. He was part of the Bilderbergers and not very well respected, as I understand it. Several military types in Poland wanted his head on a stick. Even the Pope weighed in on him."

Chase couldn't help but grin. Angelo was one of those enigmas that never ceased to amaze him. He posed as a saint but nearly always left the impression he might be up to no good and couldn't be trusted. In spite of it all, something about the guy made Chase like him.

"No clue, Vernon. Anyone else?"

"No. But you got company standing in front of the house at the edge of the driveway. Calling the police now."

CHAPTER SEVENTEEN

The kids finished up their jobs and joined Chase in the dining room. They yawned and stretched as the old regulator clock struck midnight. He glanced toward the front door and went to check the locks and the alarm system to make sure it had been activated. While he lowered the shades again, he glimpsed the kids sitting on the steps. Sean Patrick was nodding off against his brother who had already leaned against the stair railing. Heather was stretched out on the bottom step like a spoiled feline, sound asleep.

"Okay, boys. Bedtime. Up you go." He rubbed the top of their heads and pulled them to a standing position.

"Got to brush my teeth," Daniel slurred.

"Not tonight, buddy. You can brush them extra hard tomorrow." Both boys nodded their acceptance and trudged like zombies up the stairs.

Heather resembled a limp rag doll when he reached down and lifted her into his arms. Once again, she touched his heart by snuggling in close and patting his cheek. He might never be blessed enough to become a father, but he had tonight. He wasn't going to let anything spoil it.

"Boys, can you come sleep in your mom's room tonight so I can keep better tabs on you?"

For once, they didn't put up a fuss but dragged sleeping bags emblazoned with pictures of the Avengers displayed in bold colors out of a closet. They had somehow managed to slip into their pajamas, but Heather was too far gone for him to insist she change. He laid Heather on the king-size bed, and she quickly rolled onto her stomach in the middle. The boys brought a white blanket with a Disney princess from her room. After spreading the cover on her little body, he helped the boys roll out their bags on each side of their sister. They quickly zipped themselves in and faced Heather. Sean Patrick reached out and laid an arm across her back. Daniel patted her head. She had them wrapped around her little finger, too.

This was his dream family. Chase found himself offering a desperate mental prayer. "Dear God, let them be safe tonight. Protect their hearts and souls against the evil that awaits me."

He shoved the dresser in front of the door before layering on more clothes and exiting via the window. He slid down the snowy roof and managed to swing out onto the trellis then climbed down.

The snow had stopped, and stars now speckled the sky like diamonds. A breeze stirred the snow-laden branches, making them moan under the weight. No other sound reached him as he moved to the darker side of the house near the dining room window. Several spruce trees hid him in their shadow. A partial moon cast light across the snow, leaving the impression God had flipped on the spotlights.

Cold seeped into his bones, alerting him to the fact he wasn't as young as he used to be. Although very little remained in Tessa's husband's closet, he'd grabbed a lightweight sweater and hoodie. He'd found two different pairs of gloves, but neither fit his larger hands. Knowing Tessa kept stretchy knit gloves, he retrieved a pair from the dresser drawer. With the extra give in the fabric, he could wear them. He'd left his sock hat downstairs, but the hoodie would keep him warm enough.

Whoever had been standing out front had moved on. He didn't like it. Then he spotted something dark at the edge of the driveway. With stealthy movements, he approached the unknown lump sprawled facedown in the snow. A moan escaped the man wearing a Grass Valley PD uniform. Chase knelt down and rolled him over. He recognized the officer who had given him the note from Vernon.

"Officer Michaels. Can you sit up?" Chase slipped an arm under his shoulders and lifted. There was a trace of blood above his eye and a gash near the hairline.

The man rubbed his head and inspected the blood on his fingers before rubbing them in the snow. His brow wrinkled, but he quickly replaced the confused expression with a scowl.

"Got the drop on me. Your people called in saying you might need assistance. I parked my car outside the gate and decided to wait for a while to make sure there were no more ins and outs tonight. Guess this guy slipped by me."

"Chances are he was already here and waited for you to leave. Not your fault. He's looking for me."

"And who are you, anyway? I mean, really. What makes you attract trouble?"

"Maybe we can have that conversation a little later. Right now, I need your help." Chase helped him stand. "Can you walk?"

He nodded and patted his holster. "Guess he didn't need my gun."

Chase observed him closer to make sure he didn't have a concussion.

"I'm good, man. Let's find him. Where are the kids?"

Chase informed him of what he'd done to keep them safe. "Good. That should work until we get this guy."

They split up to circle the house. Chase found the garage door pried open, and it would only be a matter of seconds before the alarm went off in the house. That would either scare the kids to death or send them into ninja mode.

The thought had touched his brain when a piercing whistle alarm went off. He sped up and raced into the laundry room where he saw a tan-and-white-clad figure move into the kitchen, reach the security alarm, and punch in a series of numbers. The alarm ceased. Chase wondered how he knew this information and figured Vernon would be able to unravel that as well.

Since his entrance had not been detected, thanks to the alarm, Chase prepared to neutralize the situation quickly in case the kids were trying to move the dresser and escape the bedroom. Why hadn't he left a note taped to the door warning them not to come out, no matter what they heard?

"You've been a busy guy tonight," he growled.

The intruder stiffened his stance then slowly turned toward Chase. He lowered his head like a bull ready to charge. By the way he carried himself and showed no fear, Chase understood this beast would be an equal match. A smile spread across his lips as he narrowed his eyes. He tilted his head, releasing a loud pop from his neck.

"Whatever you want, we can do it outside." Chase glanced toward the window over the sink to indicate his wishes.

"You were a hard one to find." The man spoke with a South African accent. "Never figured you for a babysitter."

"I'm guessing there are going to be a number of things you didn't figure on tonight."

"I like a challenge."

In a blink of an eye, he pulled out a knife and hurled it at Chase who sidestepped it so that it stuck in the doorframe. Before he could react further, the man lunged at him, knocking him back against the wall. Both threw punches that met their mark on a jaw or gut, causing the other to stagger for only a second before catching a second wind.

Chase caught the man with an uppercut to the chin then kicked him backward. A wayward marble, left from earlier, met with the man's boot and propelled him to the floor between the laundry room and kitchen, but not before he pulled a smaller Walter P90 from his vest pocket. Chase stopped short and raised his hands. "Why me?"

"Don't know and don't care. It's a job. Got extra for it as long as I didn't ask too many questions."

"And who sent you?"

"That's one of the questions I wasn't supposed to ask," he said, making an awkward effort to climb to his feet. "Why are you so special anyway? You were supposed to be in Sacramento tonight. By the time I caught up with you, I had to wait for your friendly bumbling idiots to get caught by the police. If you had been where you planned, this could all have been avoided. Now there are kids in the house."

"They're asleep. They won't be a problem."

"Hope not. Be a shame to kill them, too."

A chill slithered up his back. "I'll go with you. Do what you need to do away from here."

The man screwed up his mouth in protest as he shook his head. "No. Gives you too much of a chance to take me out. I'll give you credit. You give as good as you get."

"So I've been told. Who are you, anyway?" Chase asked.

"Frosty the freakin' Snowman." He grinned. "And I take it you're not a college professor as I was led to believe."

"No." Chase raised his chin and looked down his nose at his killer. "I'm the Silent Knight."

"Like the song?" Chase nodded. The man revealed a gray smile and waved his gun at him. "Why don't you sing me a verse before you become permanently silent. Love to see the expressions on the faces of those little kids when they wake up and find you a bloody mess. Maybe I'll find a bow and put on your chest." When Chase continued to glare at him, he shouted, "Sing!"

He sang in a low growl in his throat.

"Silent night, Holy night,
All is calm, All is bright
Round yon virgin mother and child.
Holy infant so tender and mild,
Sleep in heavenly peace.
Sleep in heavenly peace, asshole."

Chase grabbed a string of Christmas lights twisted into a garland wreath on the kitchen window and tossed it to the intruder who let it fall on the floor. Because he stood in a puddle of melted snow, the lights short-circuited and sent an electric current up his leg, causing him to toss the gun. Chase caught it in midair. The man cried out as he fell back. Chase reached over and unplugged the lights then shoved the wreath aside with the toe of his boot and towered over the killer.

"Get up. You'll live. Don't make me wish I hadn't unplugged those lights."

He lay there a few seconds, trying to catch his breath then rolled to one side and eased to his knees. He looked over at Chase and threw a shoe he found on the floor at him, knocking the gun out of his hand. As he came up off the floor, Chase heard a zizzing sound, and the man started trembling again.

The police officer had slipped in behind him through the door and used his Taser gun. He managed to connect with the man's legs, sending him back to the floor. The officer finished him off with a kick to the kidneys, slamming him face-first into a wooden bench. Teeth flew out of his mouth along with blood.

"Merry Christmas," the officer said pleasantly.

CHAPTER EIGHTEEN

❦

Got a call about a stolen snowplow. You guys got some ID?" The highway patrolman with the square jaw tilted his head to the side. One eye closed almost completely. "Oh. Sorry, ma'am. Expected a man driving this thing."

Tessa felt a prickle at the back of her neck as she leaned forward to stare out the window at their car. She reached over, touched Honey's arm, and whispered, "That's not a state issued Highway Patrol car. The new ones are silver. The white ones were sold at auction last summer. Made the news."

"Who's your friend up there?" The officer didn't wait for an answer as he backed up and stretched his neck.

Honey offered a smile. "My sister. If you call this in, I'll get fired. Not supposed to have anyone ride along. I didn't want to be out the first time by myself."

"License, please." The officer moved closer to the truck. "Maybe you should get out of the truck while we check you out. I want to see your sister's license, too."

"We're screwed," Tessa mumbled in a panic.

"Sure thing. Let me see. Where did I put that? Oh, here it is." Honey leaned down and grabbed something under her seat.

"What is that? Honey, what are you going to do?" She lifted a dark object into her lap before passing papers through the window to the officer. "What are you doing? Honey…" she warned as the officer instructed them again, to get out of the truck. Both women unbuckled their seat belts, Tessa ready to scoot over to join her on the ground.

Without warning, Honey swung the door open at such speed the officer took a step back. Next, she leaped onto the door, holding herself up by propping her arms through the open window, and went with the door as it propelled outward. Before the officer could step back again, Honey moved her body out at an angle then kicked the man in the head, sending him spinning facedown in the snow. The door bounced back in, and Honey grabbed the iron bar lying on the seat before hopping down in the snow.

Another man ran around from the back of the truck, pulling his gun. Honey stood still as a mouse as he ordered her to raise her hands. Tessa knew that would be unlikely.

"I said, hands in the air!"

Honey slowly turned her head toward the new threat. Her profile mimicked a hero from a video game where all the characters were hell-bent on killing pretty much everyone. Shoulders pulled back, eyes glassy with determination to take down the enemy, Honey had moved into her killing zone.

Tessa had inched closer to watch when she accidently fell on the airhorn, startling the man into jumping and lifting a hard glare at her. The next instant, Honey hurled the iron bar at the man, knocking the gun out of his hand. Even as it connected, she ran toward him then jumped so that her body went sideways, landing both feet into his gut.

Scampering out of the truck, Tessa ran to retrieve the weapon. A bullet whizzed by her ear as a shot rang out. Without thinking, she turned and returned fire at the other man coming out of the car ahead of them.

"Let's go," she shouted. By now she knew for sure these men weren't official Nevada Highway Patrol. This new one wore desert camouflage and called for the other men on the ground to kill them. She fired again and again until Honey joined her. Without hesitation, Honey chanced relieving the first downed man of his gun then shot at the car ahead of them while Tessa climbed back into the cab and she scooted across the seat. Honey scrambled up to join her.

The engine had never been turned off. Honey put it in gear and raised the plow enough to shield against the automatic gunfire pelting the truck. She picked up speed and headed right for them, plowing into them so hard their SUV flipped over on its side. The men jumped out of the way and reloaded.

"Back it up and bury them with the plow," Tessa said.

"My thoughts exactly."

In seconds, Honey had backed up and lowered the plow blade. She hit the gas, sending a mountain of snow over the men.

Tessa spotted the first two men inching up behind them. She grabbed Honey's arm without taking her eyes from the side mirror.

"I see 'em," she growled.

The road in front of them was now blocked, and a fire flared in the overturned SUV. Turning such a big piece of equipment around quickly would be impossible. Throwing the rig into reverse and backing in top speed caused the other two to jump to the side of the road. They staggered forward. Tessa gasped at the realization they had both returned to their vehicle and retrieved shotguns, now aimed at them.

The first blast hit the front of their truck. Honey slammed on the brakes then once more put it in drive and lowered the plow before barreling toward them.

Both women burst into laughter when the men ran away like scared rabbits. Honey didn't stop until she'd thrown enough snow to neutralize them. She braked and let the truck idle a few seconds before turning to Tessa. "I don't know when I've had this much fun."

Tessa tried to contain her grin. "I'll have to agree."

They high-fived and then carefully turned the truck around to head back out to the interstate and wait out the real cops. Finding a map in the glove box, they planned another way back to Grass Valley. It wasn't impossible.

By the time they'd pulled over at an abandoned gas station, it was obvious they weren't going any farther. Steam clouds seeped out from under the hood, and the dashboard instruments indicated they were almost out of fuel.

"Hope they don't have reinforcements," Tessa said, looking out the window in the direction they'd left.

"I doubt it. No need to see if they're tracking us. Left them with few options, and they're hurt. We need another ride."

Tessa felt exhausted. Maybe this was an adrenaline rush for Honey, but all the excitement had left her drained, confused at her own behavior, and terrified of what lay ahead. Why couldn't she have listened to Chase and minded her own business at the airport? It wasn't as if he couldn't take care of himself. But the thought of her kids being in the crosshairs of a vigilante drove her to be momma bear again. Now here she was, an accomplice in at least one murder, disposal of a corpse, grand theft auto, assault on what may have been law enforcement, in possession of government property, destroying government property, and the unlawful use of a firearm. How would Christmas be spent locked up with other thugs and felons? What did it matter? Soon she would be caught, and her family would realize what a horrible person she'd become in the name of national security the last few years. Maybe President Austin would grant her a pardon.

Merry Christmas to me, she thought woefully.

"Might as well take a nap." Honey sighed.

"Who were those guys? Were they after you?"

"Not sure." She smiled, scanning the surroundings. "I make friends wherever I go."

Tessa could only groan at the response.

There was still enough juice in the truck for Honey to back it in on the far side of the gas station where they wouldn't be so easily found. Tessa stared out the window for a long time, thinking about the future without her family and how they would be disgraced and hate her. They would be raised by a father who put them second to his job, rarely get to Tennessee to visit her family, and would seek out her neighbors, the Ervins, to be the loving support they craved.

The last thing she remembered before dozing off was praying Chase could protect her children. Several hours later, she awoke to banging on the side of the truck. Both women jolted upright, grabbed their weapons, and blinked the sleep fog from their brains.

"I don't see anything." Tessa twisted in her seat to look into the night now cloaked in white snow.

Another round of loud banging, this time on Tessa's door, spiked her curiosity. She'd pushed her face against the window when a man's face appeared. With a scream, she dropped her weapon and tried to push toward Honey. Later she would remember Honey squealed in surprise, too. Heart racing, she leaned toward the window to get a better look. A certain amount of moisture on the glass prevented her from seeing clearly, but the face was familiar. She reached out and cleared the fog to see Reverend Angelo.

"Ladies, do you need a ride home?"

CHAPTER NINETEEN

Chase knew this day would come. The man who wanted him dead had finally surrounded himself with enough wealth and fame to feel invincible against the outside world. The protection was real in today's world. Money could do almost anything.

Frosty the Freakin' Snowman had been carted off to jail. When the snow stopped and the heavens cleared, Chase had managed to reach out through regular channels to get them to send a chopper to pick up the prisoner. They faced hoops to jump through to get that accomplished, thanks to the Grass Valley PD. But, in the end, they gave up the prisoner to Enigma agents who took him to the warehouse where interrogations would happen. It didn't take long to find out what he needed to know.

Goliath, as he was known in the world circles of power and influence, wanted him dead. Chase was a pesky fly in his ointment of indulgence and shady deals. The world saw him as a philanthropist, business giant, and a man who nearly walked on water. Chase knew him to be a murderer and planned to prove it. In the last few months, the captain had come across damning information to start him on his quest of revenge and justice.

He figured Goliath now knew trouble brewed for him. Better to take out the one man who wasn't afraid of him, who carried a reason to never give up. Chase's baby sister had died at the man's hands. The plan wouldn't happen overnight. Such an idea would need a lot of moving parts. For tonight, all remained safe. The man wouldn't try anything in the near future. Dealing with him would be a calculated mission for the future and through Enigma to give it justification.

For a few seconds, he thought of Tessa and whether or not to tell her about Goliath. Would the secrets he'd withheld from her from the beginning of their relationship force her to resign from Enigma? She didn't even know yet how he planned to use her in seeking revenge. This was too close for comfort tonight. If Goliath found out about Tessa, if he saw her, then all would be lost. He needed to do a better job at keeping her hidden and safe. He decided to wait to fill in the details for her. Maybe this time next year he could finish what he'd promised to do long ago.

After the police left, he went back outside and climbed in the upstairs window to find the children sound asleep. He returned the dresser to its original position before going back downstairs to finish cleaning up. It was five a.m. before he returned upstairs and found a spot on the love seat to stretch out and fall asleep. Their soft breathing and occasional mumbles lulled him to sleep. This was the best Christmas present he'd ever had.

~ ~ ~ ~

Angelo posed as a saint might stand before his God when the women joined him on the ground. Although he didn't smile, a certain amount of mischief and satisfaction danced in his hooded eyes. A few flurries drifted down to rest on hair peppered with gray. The priestly collar showed clearly since his long coat was unbuttoned. Except for his hands being locked in front of his body, for a second, he reminded Tessa of a gunslinger from the Old West, ready to do some street justice.

She stopped in front of him, and the twinkle in his eyes disappeared. He cocked his head to the side, letting his eyes go over her from top to bottom. When he straightened and dropped his hands to his side, she considered the man only posed as a man of God.

"Trouble finds you." The deep voice indicated he might know

all about her past.

"Who are you?" Tessa asked when she sensed Honey come up behind her and stand quietly.

"Tonight, I'm your guardian angel." A slow narrow smile formed on lips that looked blue in the shadows of the night.

"My car..." Her words faded as Honey moved toward the white sedan.

"Nothing to worry about. It will be in your driveway by midmorning, good as new."

"Why did you damage it?"

He fanned out his hand toward their new ride. "Who says I did? You of all people know God works in mysterious ways, especially at Christmas."

"I call shotgun. Tessa, you're in the back seat," Honey declared as she jerked the door open. "Want to make sure I keep an eye on this guy." She peered inside then looked back at Angelo, pointing to the back seat. "Who is that guy?"

Tessa pushed in front of her to take a look. In seconds, she jerked the back door open and slipped inside next to the man in handcuffs with a gag shoved in his mouth.

"Agent Martin," Tessa said, removing the gag. A bruise darkened his cheek. "Are you all right?"

"You know him?" Honey asked.

"Remember I said I recognized a man at the airport. Meet Special Agent Dennis Martin."

"Great. A conman, an FBI agent, and an assassin. Does anyone else feel like we've become the three wise men? I mean wise persons," Honey said sarcastically. "Guess you'll play the part of Mary." She reached in and slapped Tessa on the back of the head.

"And you are?" Agent Martin asked.

"Honey Lynch."

Tessa watched him roll his eyes upward and lean back against the seat. "Another one of Enigma's junkyard dogs." She was glad he said it under his breath. It would be like Honey to take offense and come over the seat at him.

"How are you involved with this, Dennis?" Tessa couldn't remember ever calling him by his first name. Maybe it would take the edge off their past encounters.

"Get me out of these cuffs now, Tessa," Agent Martin

demanded.

She eased back out of the car. "Why?" she asked, looking at Angelo who stared into the distance like a demonic creature evaluating the pits of Hell. A wave of panic engulfed her.

"We need to go. They're coming." Angelo hurried to the other side of the car and quickly slipped behind the wheel.

"W-who's coming?" Tessa stuttered even as she rejoined the FBI agent in the back seat.

Honey buckled up as Angelo spun out and headed back toward the interstate then took a surprising turn away on a side road.

"Who are we running from?" Tessa tried to touch the back of Angelo's seat, but the seat belt held her tight.

"Angelo stole a lot of money from a drug kingpin and now is running for his life," Agent Martin interjected.

"It was for military families who needed a little extra help." His voice sounded like he might be practicing for an interview on the evening news. "Agent Martin had the misfortune of getting in my way. After I saw him getting out of your car at the casino, I had to bring him along before he notified the authorities. I wasn't sure I could trust him." He gave a jovial laugh. "Funny how things work out. Now here we are, one big happy family."

Tessa had been in similar circumstances with Agent Martin. Shifty eyes, blank expression when he talked to you, attempting to rid the world of corruption, one bad guy at a time. There wasn't much wiggle room with him. Black and white were his favorite colors in everything he did, especially concerning his work. He was part of her history now, thanks to Enigma, she felt obligated to protect him.

"When I told him I had to help you tonight, Agent Martin decided he would be more than happy to tag along."

"Do I look happy to you?" the agent snarled.

Tessa reached over and laid her comforting hand on his arm, only to have him shake it off.

"You know the police are looking for you, right?" he continued.

"Not to worry, Tessa." Angelo adjusted the rearview mirror and adjusted it to see her image. "I will get you to your children."

"Wait. How did you know about my kids?"

Honey raised her gun and jabbed it into Angelo's arm. "I was wondering the same thing."

"Maybe a little Christmas music will relax everyone," he said turning on the radio.

"Maybe if you stop driving like a bat out of hell, we'd all relax." Honey poked him again.

"We Three Kings" performed by the New York Philharmonic, started him singing at the top of his lungs. Tessa had to admit he sang quite well. She glanced over at Agent Martin who glared at her with the slow simmering rage she'd seen before when they had tangled.

"Why were you at the airport, Dennis?"

"It's Agent Martin to you, and none of your business."

Angelo turned down the radio and glanced to the mirror at his passengers. "He was looking for me. You caused a stir in the airport looking for your best friend—"

"She's not my best friend."

Honey turned back to look at her. "Why do you continually try and hurt my feelings, after all we've been through?

"You're kinda the reason we went through it," she snapped, making eye contact with Angelo again.

"Anyway, you provided me with a chance to slip away. I spotted Agent Martin getting out of his car. He saw you and actually crossed the street, I guessed to follow you." Angelo made the sign of the cross on his chest. "Thank you, baby Jesus, for helping me escape."

"Baby Jesus had nothing to do with your escape," Agent Martin fumed. "You recognized me because I'd been on your tail for a month. Nearly caught you in LA two days earlier. I did follow Tessa because I got word a woman had been seen with you minutes before. When I saw her crossing to the parking garage, I figured the way trouble follows her around, the two of you had to be connected."

"Yes. But you lost her in the garage."

"And you tried to run me over."

"I didn't see you." Angelo smiled up at the rearview mirror.

"Whatever, Angelo." He turned back to Tessa. "I hurried back to my car and spotted you leaving and noticed someone else was with you. I thought it might be Captain Hunter, so I caught up with you. When you parked at the casino, I realized my mistake and had my men go back to the airport."

"And you followed me inside."

"No. I waited to see what you might be planning. When it looked like you were leaving. I found your car."

Tessa gasped then slapped his thigh.

"Sorry, by the way, for the damage on your car. I thought you might get away. Imagine my surprise when I saw Angelo with you. That's when I knew I had to delay your departure."

"So, you weren't looking for me?" Honey asked.

"No. But now I can take both of you in together."

Honey and Angelo looked at each other and burst out laughing. When they caught their breath, Angelo found a place to pull in before getting back on the highway. They were far from the checkpoint to cross over into California now, and it appeared the snowplows had done a good job making it passable. After unbuckling his seat belt, he turned to look at his passengers.

"That is nonsense, Agent Martin. This is what you're going to do. You are going to make sure Tessa and Honey are never associated with what may or may not have happened in Reno in the last ten hours. And, in return, I will give up the Russian oligarch I stole the money from by giving you his location and his plans for the next week. I'm sure my information will put him away for a very long time. Honey, I'm sure, will have a treat to offer as well, but it is her decision to make."

"And I'm sure you want something in return."

"I want only to see law and order...well, and the money I have taken from the Russian. He has plenty more, and I can provide the outlets for money laundering he uses. It would be frosting on the cake. That should make you quite the rock star at headquarters."

Tessa reached out to touch Agent Martin's arm, but he pulled away before she could make contact. "Please, Agent Martin. I will so owe you, big-time!" She grabbed his cuffed hands. "I would never survive in jail. Doesn't all I've done for the country mean anything? You and I have been through so much together and..."

"Oh stop," he moaned. "You have become the manipulating little mouse Enigma hoped you'd become when they signed you up." He held out his hands. "And stop with the fake tear at the corner of your eye and get me out of these. It's a deal. But if Angelo and your Irish buddy don't come through for me, you're toast."

Angelo passed Tessa the key so she could free him. Before he could adjust to a more comfortable position, she hugged him then landed a kiss on his cheek. He frowned at her and made a big effort to show his irritation by wiping it away.

"You're a menace, Tessa Scott." He rubbed his wrists before leveling a look of contempt toward Honey who watched him like an angry wolverine. "Why were you two teamed up anyway? I thought you ran with a better class of people. And you." He snarled at Honey with a crooked lip. "Where's my weapon by the way?"

The agent was baiting a dangerous woman, hoping to force her into an out-of-control rage so he could still haul her off to jail. Clicking her seat belt, she leaned forward to get him focused on her again.

"I'll give it back when we return to Grass Valley." Honey smiled.

Tessa tried to get his attention by snapping her fingers in front of his nose to distract him from glaring at Honey like he was ready to cuff and mirandize her. "She found out there was a hit out on Hunter. It was supposed to happen tonight."

"So? He's a big boy. I'm sure he can take care of himself. Can't be anything new for him."

"Well, he was babysitting my kids," Tessa said. "We tried to warn him in time. But you never know what my kids could be exposed to. They could also get hurt."

Agent Martin pursed his lips and pointed to Honey. "This is probably your fault. I'm keeping you on my radar."

She narrowed her eyes and blew him a kiss. If the woman wanted to, she could climb over the back seat and land a killing blow to his throat faster than he could lean back. No doubt she would give him a passionate kiss on the mouth before he died. Tessa put her hand on Honey's shoulder and squeezed gently, drawing her death stare to her. It softened immediately.

"Don't pay him any attention. Okay?"

Honey nodded and turned away. "Okay."

Angelo laid his hand on his heart. "I feel like God has brought a miracle right here before us this night."

In unison, the other three groaned as Angelo started the car.

CHAPTER TWENTY

Chase opened one eye when the first rays of morning pierced the sheer curtains in Tessa's bedroom. He noticed immediately the boys had dragged their sleeping bags onto the floor in front of him. Heather had climbed up in his lap and laid her head against his chest. Instinctively, he wrapped his arms around her and kissed her curly head. A fleeting thought of Tessa touched his brain. He hoped she had gotten the message that all was well on the home front and not to worry. In seconds, he fell back asleep, knowing this little domestic scene would soon be replaced by his real world.

~ ~ ~ ~

The four unlikely partners in crime had to pull over three more times to wait for the snowplow to clear enough road for them. From Reno to Grass Valley was less than one hundred miles over the mountains. It should have taken only about an hour and a half to cross over, but with the snow and unexpected distractions, they were coming up on eight hours. The sun rose and intermittent streams of light sliced through the billowy clouds and seemed blinding at times.

After a call came through, Angelo willingly handed Tessa her stolen cell phone. "It was for your own good," he explained.

The news had been good. Chase and the children were safe, and the hitman had been captured, according to Vernon Kemp. He relayed how he'd been trying to track them all night and put in place a few roadblocks of the cyber kind to help if she needed it. She informed him Agent Martin was with her along with Honey Lynch. She thought it best not to mention Angelo.

Shortly after, the director of Enigma entered the conversation and asked to speak to Agent Martin. The two of them talked the rest of the way to Grass Valley and sounded like they'd come to an understanding concerning the night's events.

A calm washed over her as they neared her subdivision, now a winter wonderland filled with beautiful snow. She couldn't wait to hold her babies and tell them how much she loved them. Hopefully, they wouldn't require therapy after wondering where their mother might be or having to suffer the drill sergeant mentality of Captain Hunter. He wasn't used to compromise, and he certainly didn't know anything about kids. But she had trusted him nonetheless, to stay a couple of hours so she could pick up her parents. There had been no way of knowing how the events would shift everything.

When she got out of the car in her driveway, Honey joined her. "Here's your keys. The only one missing is your car key. Angelo says he had to give it to the repair man to drive back." The two women tried to avoid eye contact and ran the toes of their boots through the snow.

"Thanks for being my wingman, Tessa. You're all right."

"Merry Christmas, Honey. I guess you're okay, too."

The two women embraced. Tessa quickly checked to see if the woman had lifted anything from her pockets, drawing a smile from the assassin before she slipped back inside the car. Tessa leaned down to wink at Angelo then gave a thumbs-up to Agent Martin. They'd already said their goodbyes, and it was probably a good idea not to let them tarry too long.

After punching in the security code and letting herself in, Tessa quickly turned off the alarm and looked around the house. It was immaculate. She moved through the rooms quietly, knowing everyone probably continued to sleep. Besides the dining room window having cardboard taped over the outside, the only thing that looked a little out of place was a string of garland and some

Christmas lights in the trash. She pulled them out only to notice they were charred black. The back door also looked as if it had undergone some repairs.

After a few minutes, she headed upstairs and was surprised the children weren't in their rooms. Walking into her room, she found Chase's body half on and half off the small love seat and the children asleep in various positions near him. With his head propped up on one of her chenille pillows, someone—probably Heather—had managed to place a pink sparkly tiara, at an angle, on his head. The feathers of a purple boa wrapped around his neck moved each time he exhaled. He held Heather in one arm, and the other hand gripped one of the boys' light sabers.

Tessa grabbed her phone and took several pictures of the scene. She'd frame the best one and give it to Chase for Christmas. She stared at them a few more minutes before reaching down and touching the boys who woke immediately.

"Mom!" they chorused and scrambled up into her arms. She kissed them and tousled their hair.

Heather awoke and tried to climb down. Chase opened his eyes. Tessa leaned over Chase, lifted her daughter into her arms, and squeezed. "How's my girl?"

"Good. We had so much fun, Mommy."

"Really? How about you boys?"

They nodded and talked at the same time about a few exploits that sounded more than a little concerning to her. By now, Chase had sat up and yawned.

"Mimi and Poppy should be on their way from the airport. They had to fly into Sacramento because of the weather. So, I missed them. Sorry it took so long." The last comment had been intended for Chase. "Tell you what. How about I fix everyone some breakfast in a few minutes. Go change your clothes and clean up. Okay?"

Their exit sounded like galloping horses as she turned her eyes back on Chase who rubbed tired eyes and stretched.

"Do you realize you're wearing a tiara and a purple boa?"

"I'm getting in touch with my princess side."

Tessa couldn't help but offer a light laugh. "I see. Is this a career move?"

"Hell no. This is too hard. I'm giving you a raise after

Christmas and more time off. I'm exhausted. Several hours ago, they got up, and Heather demanded we still have our princess school. I agreed, if they'd go lie down for a few hours afterward. I'm not wearing any lipstick, am I?"

She tugged at his outstretched hand to pull him up. Turning his face this way and that, she then grabbed a tissue off the dresser and brushed it across his cheek. "All good now. Thank you for taking such good care of them. Anything you want to share with me before they start giving me a play-by-play of last night's activities?"

"Not really. Anything I need to know about the last twelve hours or so with you?" Chase rubbed his eyes and yawned.

Tessa shrugged and fluffed a Christmas tree pillow on the love seat. "No. I can't think of anything." She smiled up at him.

"Oh, I did have to repair your back door. And I folded three baskets of laundry. I also ran the vacuum and organized your pantry."

"You're sweet-talkin' me now."

A grin toyed with the corner of one side of his mouth. "Yes, I am."

Tessa stood on tiptoe and kissed him on the mouth. "Thank you. Maybe there is something I can do for you."

That steamy look she so loved in his dark eyes appeared but quickly evaporated as he moved toward the bedroom door. "I'm too tired. And I may have a headache. I need coffee."

She started to laugh and rub his back.

"Come on. I'll help you cook breakfast. I want to make sure the kids get their stories straight. Then, after I get a nap, and if you still want to thank me, we'll talk."

THE END

MEET TIERNEY JAMES

Tierney James decided to become a full-time writer after working in education for over thirty years. Besides serving as a Solar System Ambassador for NASA's Jet Propulsion Lab, and attending Space Camp for Educators, Tierney served as a Geo-teacher for National Geographic. Her love of travel and cultures took her on adventures throughout Africa, Asia and Europe. From the Great Wall of China to floating the Okavango Delta of Botswana, Tierney weaves her unique experiences into the adventures she loves to write. Living on a Native American reservation and in a mining town, fuels the characters in the Enigma and Wind Dancer series.

After moving to Owasso, Oklahoma the love of teaching continued in her marketing and writing workshops along with the creation of educational materials and children's books. Try some of her other books to bring a little adventure to your life. http://www.tierneyjames.com Speaking at book clubs, school functions, church and community groups are a few of the things Tierney enjoys doing when not writing her next adventure. She also helps beginning writers in their quest to becoming a published author through her workshops and classes.

Invisible Goodbye – Enigma 7

Chapter 1

Darkness always felt eternal flying over the ocean at night. The lights were dimmed several hours earlier. Most passengers fell asleep in spite of the twenty minutes of turbulence earlier in the flight. The occasional flash of distant lightning was the only evidence the plane remained at 34,000 feet. This somehow comforted Joel Sandy as he clicked on the video screen embedded in the back of the seat in front of him.

He'd always enjoyed watching the flight path of the plane as it moved along the lines of latitude on the virtual map. Noting the wind speed, altitude, weather forecast and various other statistics most of his friends ignored, gave him pleasure and a certain amount of comfort that all was right with this part of the world.

Since he had an aisle seat, he stretched out one of his long legs, then eased out to stand up and use the restroom one more time before slipping on his comfy socks to put him in the mood. He could feel the antihistamine he'd taken an hour earlier start to take effect. When he returned to his seat, he fished out the sleep mask provided to all first-class ticket holders.

For a few seconds he felt his body tilt to the right as if the plane made a turn. He glanced at the screen again to check their location. The plane was gently moving away from the route he'd expected in order to reach their morning stop in Dubai. He pushed the call button.

"Yes, sir?" The flight attendant had boarded the plane ahead of the passengers. He noticed her and that she didn't look so much like someone from Singapore, but maybe Central Asia. "I didn't expect you to still be awake?" Her smile seemed a little taunt.

"According to this map, we are turning north. Is there a problem?"

"Not at all. Just an adjustment. There's a storm up ahead and the pilot wishes to avoid any turbulence."

Suddenly the plane bounced as if it were losing altitude. "Something is wrong."

"Please buckle up. I'll go check it out."

Even as he kept an eye on the plane moving across the map, sleep caressed his fears until his eyelids began to feel heavy. He spotted the flight attendant talking to someone who appeared to be the pilot. She pointed toward Joel and the pilot eased down the aisle and squatted down by him. The attendant followed.

"I think it is okay. He's almost out." The pilot stood and smiled at the attendant. "This will soon be over."

Joel tried to call out to the others, but his voice wouldn't work, or the rest of his body. Had he been poisoned or medicated? With his sight starting to fade he watched the small airplane on the map disappear just before the screen went dark. They were going to crash.

~ ~ ~ ~

President Buck Austin was just sitting down for a late lunch with his guests, the ambassadors from Western Europe. He'd decided they needed a "Come to Jesus" speech about their support of NATO and their monetary contributions. The United Nations Ambassador, Talala Anderson, also attended to make her case for greater support for sanctions against Russia, Iran and North Korea.

The president's Chief of Staff entered and bent down to whisper in his ear. He stood and motioned for everyone to begin eating. Something needed his attention and would return as soon as possible.

"Just give it to me straight," he ordered in his no nonsense manner when irritated.

The Chief of Staff remained standing as the president leaned against his desk in the Oval Office and crossed his arms. "A plane went missing several hours ago on its flight from Singapore. About twenty of the two hundred passengers were Americans."

"Was it a terrorist attack?" The president knew he should be use to this kind of thing, but it never got easy, knowing precious lives were lost due to some crazed individual who had no respect for human life.

"We are just getting information. The Pentagon has been alerted, sir."

"The Pentagon? Why? What are you not telling me?" The president straightened and frowned.

"Those twenty Americans were some of our best scientists and engineers. They were working with DARPA and the Pentagon on a revolutionary cloaking device for our military aircraft and body armor for combat. The project was nearing completion. Several traveled to Singapore for a conference and some of the others were visiting relatives in neighboring countries. They were also guest lecturers at universities. All of them met up yesterday to return back to the States and their work."

"Are they the only ones working on this project?" The president knew he should care more about the possible loss of life than a protected government project—but he didn't. "And did it not occur to anyone at DARPA sending twenty scientists and engineers to Asia was a bad idea? Sometimes I think they don't have enough sense to wad a shotgun," he complained in his Texas accent.

"Yes sir. They were working in conjunction with DARPA but not exclusively. Jango International Aeronautics, out of New Mexico was contracted through the Pentagon for this project."

"Then we didn't lose everyone?"

The Chief of Staff checked his notes. "We don't know yet, Mr. President."

"Then find someone who does know," he shouted. "Someone is going to pay for this screw up. This is what I want to know; what happened to that plane, who was responsible, and who the hell let so many brains leave the country? Am I clear?"

"Yes, Mr. President."

"And when you find the idiot who let them leave, drag his ass in here so I can rip him a new one. And I want all that by tonight," he fumed as he walked to the door. "Now I'm going to have a nice lunch and suggest our so called 'allies', get ready for some trouble. Hopefully, that plane is at the bottom of the ocean and not in some third world hell-hole selling our people to the highest bidder."

"Mr. President, if they are still alive, what will be your orders?"

The president stopped as his hand squeezed the doorknob. He looked down at the floor then back at the Chief of Staff. "The official report will be that they all died. Do you understand?"

The Chief of Staff raised his chin and paled. "Are you sure, Mr. President?"

The president pulled back his shoulders and opened the door. "Do it."

Printed in the USA
CPSIA information can be obtained
at www.ICGtesting.com
CBHW051928221024
16238CB00015B/851